★ TEENAGE ★

★ IDOL ★

★ TEENAGE ★

★ IDOL ★

J. Merridew

I dedicate this book
to my teenage idols.
I loved you endlessly,
but all you ever gave me
was a terrible feeling
of insecurity.

Go to hell.

<u>Featuring:</u>

The Deep End

On City Limits

Bleach, Blood & Cum

Brutus: Part One

Suburbia

Solo Cups & Bruises: Part Two

Lax Hoes, Sports Bros

Trophy Boy: Part Three

The Deep End

I have brown eyes and brown hair. When I'm alone on Friday nights, I comb my hair like Jimmy used to and smoke sugar cigarettes. I look at myself in the mirror until my vision goes blurry. It's not because I like what I see, but because I'm trying to see what everyone else does. They all tell me that I'm special and beautiful, and it's flattering of course, but I just want to see it for myself.

This world is beautiful. Really, it is. I love all things, but my favorites are rusted bubblegum machines and the scent of your hair on my pillowcase. People admire my confidence, but they never see me when I'm alone. That's when I'm the most raw because I'm not trying to sell myself to anybody.

I'm just a boy. Nothing more and nothing less. People like to think that I'm special, but you can't see the moments that make me just like you because I don't let you in that far.

I'm in love with what the American dream used to be. I'm in love with girls who wear ribbons in their curls and boys who bleed in black and white. I can't stop watching J.F.K. lose his brains and

I'm fascinated with plane crashes and dead pin-ups. I'm just obsessed with finding out why the nights are darker in America.

I want you to question everything that you see. Question what I'm selling you because you bought into my world and there is a *reason.* Something about me is resonating somewhere inside of you because you wouldn't be reading this right now if you didn't believe in it. If you aren't here because of a pretty face or overly-edited photograph, then you're exactly where I want you to be. We're both lonely in the head, but we've made it.

We've made it, kid.

I taste sweet, like American candy bars. When you get me going, I taste salty too. Sweet and salty like chocolate-covered pretzels.

You said that you fell in love with me the moment that you saw me. Maybe it's because I look like hope and you haven't really seen that in a while. I promise that you will never meet another boy like me. I embrace the darkness that you've fought so strongly to blind with your camera flashes. I am broken down in such an artistic, artificial way.

But I wasn't always that way.

Before I got in deep, my skin wasn't clear and my eyes were lighter. My cheek bones were less prominent and my nose didn't fit my face as well as it does now. The sun didn't shine across my skin, it just ruined it. My hair was curly on the ends and cropped all wrong.

All of that changed when I met him. He made me feel strange in such a remarkable way that I couldn't even begin to explain. I gave him everything that I had and he gave me everything that I've ever wanted. He listened to me. Nobody ever listens to me the way he did.

There will come a day when you meet the person who offers you the world. It'll be such a beautiful day, and you'll think that things are finally going to be okay because he'll take away your tears and you'll be happy for the first time since you swung on the swings back in grade school and got mulch in your shoes.

Don't you remember those days? Don't you miss them?

"I want to be a *star*," I cried, wiping tears from my eyes.

He brought a hand to my face and stroked my cheek. A shiver crawled down my spine like spiders along the wall when nobody is awake to see them.

Some people just sparkle. They glitter like gold, but my head was never heavy with the crown and it wasn't fair. It was my turn. It was about time that I got everything that I ever wanted because I deserved something.

I needed to do it. Don't leave me. Don't hate me. It's just… big dreams don't mix well with small towns. They never have and never will. I just want to run this world, but that doesn't mean, even for a moment, that I'm a drugged-up failure with syringes full of attention and fished-up compliments. No, I don't get high off of attention. That's not what this is about. I just judge my self-worth by how many people know my name.

And now, he knows it too.

When I first met him, I wasn't in a good place. I spent my summer nights swimming laps in my pool and drinking Coca Cola during sunset. For weeks, all I could taste was chlorine and it burned my eyes, but I kept swimming because I wanted the body of the boys who have gold medals on the television.

Back and forth I went. My lungs felt like grocery bags that get caught in tree branches during storms. I was crying while I swam, but nobody noticed because it was too dark outside and nobody was there to notice even if it were light. I kept swimming until night fell and I was alone beneath millions of taunting stars.

I hoisted myself from the water before drying myself and walking upstairs to my room. I brushed my teeth and spit out blood from my gums and then turned on the light and television and went to bed.

That wasn't a typo.

And when I finally fell asleep, I had an awful dream that I was somebody's dream. And when I woke up and realized that it wasn't real, I started crying. I pulled the Jimmy posters from my wall and ripped them apart. I scratched away Ricky's eyes and broke Marilyn's frame.

I screamed and dragged it all outside, where I tossed it into the pool because I wanted to bury it all ten feet under. The broken frames floated to the top like a ship wreck, but the poster boys and pin-ups started to disintegrate and fall apart like sandcastles on an empty beach during high-tide.

The pool light wasn't on anymore and the water looked like ink. It looked threatening and terrifying. I kept crying because I was so sick of being insignificant. Just when I was about to smoke a cigarette, I heard such an awful sound bubbling up from the deep end.

I'll never know where he came from. He rose up so eerily and slowly from the black water that my breath left my lungs. When I first saw his eyes dancing above the water's surface, I thought that he was too beautiful to be real. I always thought I knew what he looked like, but the moment that I saw him, I knew that I was wrong.

He was very hard to see in the darkness. I knew that I should have been afraid that he had been swimming in my pool in the dead of night, but I was so happy to see him that I couldn't possibly be upset.

His smooth voice drifted throughout the summer air. I could barely hear it over the humming of the pool filter and the crickets. "Why are you crying?"

"I want to be a *star*."

"A star? What kind of star?"

"The kind that people put on their walls and dream about at night."

"It must be wonderful," he told me, "to be a dream."

"Oh, yes!" I said. "It must be *wonderful*."

My voice drifted across the open air like perfume. He walked closer to me until he was inches away from my bare chest. I could've sworn that the stars lost their shine because his eyes were stealing their twinkle.

He and I could've written such a beautiful story together. There would have been laughter and that melancholy chill that only means that the heart is finally beating for two.

We could've been perfect.

But I'm not interested in writing the next big romance. I'm not interested in writing novels about nerds meeting popular kids, or teenage vampires who conceive children on fantastical islands.

I'm interested in telling the story *exactly* the way it is intended, and unfortunately for me, my romance isn't between me and somebody beautiful and captivating.

My romance is between me and the devil.

And it's awfully sad how I talked to him that night while he was swimming in that murky, pool water. It's terribly unsettling how he promised me everything when I stood on the edge of the concrete, staring into the black water with such a fake glint of naivety in my eyes.

And I find it funny how I gave him my heart and he laughed and vanished forever in the water, smirking and thinking that he'd fooled me.

"I can give you the *world*," he whispered in my ear.

"That's all I've ever wanted," I cried. "I want to be a fantasy. I want to be a pin-up. I want boys to admire me and girls to dream about me and I want to have it all because I'm so terrified of dying and superstars never die, they just stop living."

"We all want infinity."

I nodded. "Oh, I'd just *love* that."

He took a few steps forward. He began feeling around my chest. His hands felt like October winds. His touch was refreshing and cold.

"What are you doing?"

"Giving you everything you've ever wanted."

A few final tears glided down my reddened, worn-out cheeks. "Do you promise?"

"Of course," he breathed. His stale breath made the hairs on my arms rise and fall like cornstalks in the wind. He grabbed hold of my hand and led me into the shallow end of the swimming pool. The water licked at my arms in such an uncomfortable way, but I followed him as he pulled me further and further into the deep end.

"Do you trust me?" he asked, his voice a hush.

I paused.

"*Always.*"

And he smiled and put his hands on me again. He told me to take off my clothes and I listened.

I'm not sure if I screamed that night. I'll never know what really happened while I was fumbling around in the deep end, gasping for breath in twelve feet of water that kept forcing its way down my throat. I couldn't see or feel and I was bleeding in places where I was never meant to bleed. And, despite all of this happening, I'll never tell you what he did to me that night.

Ever.

Nobody will ever know what the devil did to me in the deep end.

When I crawled out of the pool again, naked and crying, I hurried back inside my house and collapsed into my bed. I cried for hours and watched old cartoons because they felt like home in a world that felt so black.

The devil laughed and vanished forever in the dark water, leaving nothing behind but markings on my body. When I awoke the next morning, my cuts and scrapes had healed over. When I looked in the mirror, my eyes were darker and my eyebrows were less crooked. My teeth were the perfect size for my mouth and my hair was slicked up in the front like all the poster boys.

I was finally beautiful.

And when I logged onto my computer, I laughed because I was finally selling.

My eyes swam over to my reflection. I ran a finger across my smooth face and started laughing again until my rib cage felt misplaced and my stomach felt popped. I tossed on a black tank top, propped up a twenty dollar webcam and started recording a shitty video that he promised would hit over 100 thousand views in less than a year.

Those video views aren't an accident. They're a deal.

He gave me everything that night, but I was going to play him for such a fool. The man in black can always be fooled.

Always.

And it's hysterical how the devil was so wrong in believing that everyone who wants fame is egotistical and self-absorbed. He preys on the weak, but he never stops to wonder if you and I have had a plan from the very beginning.

As my laugh echoed throughout the empty bedroom, I knew that the man in black was going to regret giving me the world. I wasn't going to use the fame for television spots or red carpets.

No, I was going to use my fame to make sure nobody soaks their living room carpet with blood ever again. Because those are the red carpets that I'm obsessed with- the ones that you hear about on the news after the football games on Friday nights, all those stories of the boys and girls who are just going to be vintage film someday in archived news reports under the headline, "TEENAGE TRAGEDY."

We'll do it together. You and I. You'll lose those dark thoughts about who you are, and you'll leave behind those ideas that the man in black owns your love.

Because God owns me and He always will, and the devil could never change that, no matter how wide he spreads my name. Not even when my words travel oceans and climb over borders.

I am the American dream. When I bleed, it's *awfully* red, and when I bruise, it's bluer than the heavens, and I promise that you'll get lost somewhere in the whiteness of my smile.

On City Limits

I can be him. I can be yours. I can be anything. Let me be everything. Just take me to the limits. Let's make our nocturnal vows now, when they're pure. Take me to the end of the road, where the orange lights flicker and the truck horns ring like church bells. We can pass the burger stand along the way. We can dream about how we used to sit for hours and talk beneath neon beer signs.

We can run right to the limits and blur the shades. We can toe the lines of what's right and wrong. We can run past the big, red billboard and mock commercial America. We can kiss, sing, dance and dream and maybe even re-paint the yellow lines on the highway.

Take me with you, wherever you go. Take me to the city limits. Take me there. Please, just take me there.

I don't care if I'm a red boy and you're a white girl. I don't care that I have red skin and red eyes that contrast so greatly with your white cheeks and snowy eyebrows. I don't care about these red streets and buildings that raised me to be this… this *cardboard cutout*. All I want to do is throw paint on the concrete. I want Mom to yell at me. I want Dad to kick me out of the house. I want to listen to Rock and Roll and dance around my house with an air guitar. I want to break my red stop signs (and your white ones too). I want to be chased out of Mr. Stinner's yard and spend Thursday nights watching the girl next door through her window while she's changing.

I just want to be *bad*. I want to grease my red hair back and carry a comb around all the time. I want to wear ripped jeans and studded belts and blow smoke in everyone's face while laughing because they'll all try to stop us, but they'll never be able to *catch* us. We'll keep running until we're out of sight, over flower gardens and through crystal rivers.

I hate everything about the laws. I want to write my own. If they try to stop me, I'll leave in handcuffs and they'll leave on a stretcher. I'm not a good guy. I'm just… I'm just a *rotten* kid.

And I want to meet in your white gardens. I want you to come into my red ones. I want to live in a free world where we can be bad and nobody can do anything about it.

If you love me, let's run away. You can leave behind your white cars. I can leave behind the chipped, red paint of my pick-up truck. We can hop aboard the railroad or hitchhike like… like *filthy* drunkards. Nobody has to see what we do. Your white clothing can get all muddy. You don't have to wear any at all if you don't want to.

They say that we can't marry. They say that we can't be together because we don't mix. They've never seen us. They've never seen us mix color anyway, so how would they know?

Do you remember the first time we met? Do you remember when we saw each other on that playground between our two neighborhoods? There were beautiful weeping willows growing all around that splintery mess. There was a long band of black that ran down the middle of the mulch, splitting the red side from the white. The red kids played on the red swings. The white kids played on the white swings. Everything on the red side was red; from the monkey bars to the overflowing trash can that spilled ketchup wrappers and Coca Cola bottles. You could see my red neighborhood behind it, looking so fiery in the setting sun. I could see your white one too, looking so snowy and peaceful.

Do you remember the seesaw? It was so old and broken despite seeming so new and innovative. One seat was white and the other was red. That was where we fell in love. That was where we sat for hours laughing and, for the first time, holding hands. You said you wanted to kiss me. I said you were pretty. We thought each other were cool.

And there was that one weeping willow that gave us the idea. It was the largest of them all with thousands of red leaves blowing in the breeze. And do you remember what it was doing?

It was spilling over onto the white side.

You left that night- back to your chalky white home. I left to my blood red one. I couldn't forget about your pretty hair, or your soft, white lips.

I could see trucks on the highway as I went North, coughing black smoke into the night air. They carried ketchup to the red side and mayonnaise to the white. They carried tomatoes to the red markets and onions to the white.

I jumped in shock when I heard a loud crash. A truck going North crashed into a truck going South and everything inside of them intertwined. It was so beautiful, more than anyone will ever know. It was so… so *perfect* because the two colors made something I had never seen before.

They made pink.

Pink oozed across the overgrown grass and onto the side of the road. It coated the discarded cigarette packs and empty beer bottles. It made the ugly look so beautiful.

We met on the limits every night in October. You had to cheer at your high school's football games. I had to play in mine. We'd intertwine our colored fingers. When we'd steal a quick glance down, our fingers seemed to make pink again… but only for a moment.

I kept greasing my red hair back. I kept wearing a red jacket with red jeans and a belt that made me look really… really *scummy.*

You wore your white shirt and rolled up your skirt really high. You ripped your stockings and pulled the sleeves from your shirt.

Together, we were two bad kids. We were different colors. We meshed together, but we looked so *bad*. We came from these… these *beautiful* suburban homes, but that wasn't what we wanted. We didn't want beauty. We wanted reality. People watched us share a cigarette. You watched to me try to sing the classics. You'd dance in the mulch and laugh with snorts that just made us both laugh harder.

One day, we left that playground together- on the red side. We danced along the roads and ignored the looks from the passing cars. They honked their horns. They shouted slurs at us.

You looked so beautiful. Your white skin, clothing and hair contrasted with the red brick and wood of the houses in my neighborhood.

We were awful. We were bad. We were… we were Rock and Roll.

I told you that we could make it work. We could make it all work. We could redraw the boundaries and rewrite the future.

People are so misunderstanding that it breaks my heart.

They called us a lot of names. The red boys tackled me to the ground and told me that I was going to hell. They punched my face in because you were a white and I was a red. They spat on me and carved a cross in my arm. Red leaked across the street and settled into oily puddles.

The girls pulled your hair. They called you by your color. They threw stones at you and made you bleed with their nails, and when they did, your blood leaked across the pavement too. I saw your blood mixing with mine and it stunned me to silence. It caught me so off guard because you bled red, just like me.

I bled red. You bled it too. Isn't it amazing how we all bleed the same color? Maybe we're a lot more alike than we think.

We still met on the limits after that. You told me to start carrying around a pocketknife. You said you were afraid to cross over into red territory again because of what happened last time, but we had *faith*. We had faith in the fact that people can change and learn to see with shut eyes.

Once again, we broke the rules like the bad kids we were born to be.

The white gardens in your backyard were beautiful. The white leaves of the trees speckled the ground like hundreds of snowflakes. We laid in those flowers forever. We kissed for the first time and listened to the sound of the water fountain spilling into the bottom basin with a ring. You said you thought I was cool. I said I thought you were too.

Nobody caught us that night. The cops that patrol the borders were distracted with a gunman at the corner store. In those moments, we could be sinners. We could be outlaws. In those moments, we were living above the law and we were in love with each other's colored coats.

My Mom would yell at me for coming home late. I'd argue with her and say that I was old enough to make my own decisions. When she went to bed with Dad, I'd sneak through the window and run to the borderline of everything I knew.

We'd jump from one side to the other, laughing at the people living under their red and white roofs of security. We'd pick red and white flowers and toss them onto the freeway. The next day, I'd see the police guards on the red side had buried the white ones. I could only imagine the same thing was happening in white territory.

At night, I'd wake my Mom because the heavy metal I was listening to would shake the house. I'd get so into the music, I'd break the records and crack holes in my door. When Mom would complain, I'd tell her I was just a kid. She'd say I was going through a phase. I said that if I was, I wanted it to last forever.

You and I would kiss on the lips a lot- especially in the car. You'd have white boots on and white leather. I started wearing a white band around my wrist- something that was forbidden in red territory. We'd steam up the windshield. We'd draw hearts and peace signs on the moist windows with different-colored fingers.

Nobody saw us. Nobody heard us. Even then, we felt like we were living on the edge. We felt like nobody could touch us because the shots gave us warm, bubbly stomachs. We stole bottles from our parents before meeting at the playground.

One day, we proved our love for each other like true artists. You were holding my hand, running along the side of the road with me in red territory. You had just eaten spaghetti and meatballs for the first time. I snuck some from my home and we ate it in the large backyards behind the trees.

We kissed. There was a group of red boys walking on the other side of the road. They gave us the finger. They shouted awful insults and told us they were going to kill us.

I told them to try.

One of the boys, the biggest, came at me. He had deep, red tattoos on his bicep of snakes. They looked like deep veins running up his arm. He swung at me. He grabbed hold of my neck and pulled me into a headlock.

And I still had that pocketknife- the one you told me to carry around with me. I pulled it from my pocket and ran it up his arm. He shouted in pain. The red snake spilled blood into the air that rained down around us. He kept bleeding like a fountain. It was beautiful. It mixed with the dirt on the street and made such a beautiful color.

The other boys took off running. They were running to their homes and then to call the police. I knew we were outlaws now because we had spilled blood on the side of the road.

You had an idea. You dipped your pearly fingers inside that boys burst arm and stomach. You smeared the blood all down your legs and across your shoulders. I helped you paint around your eyes. I helped you coat that beautiful face of yours with that deep blood.

We were true artists now. We were true, *forbidden* artists. We were rock stars. We were bad kids.

The blood got even darker when it started to clot around your eyebrows. It dripped down your white skirt in rolls and clung to the leather. We kept painting your blank canvas until you looked like a rose.

You were red now. You were my reflection.

We continued holding hands. We strolled around the red neighborhood and swung side by side on the swings. We shared a cigarette, danced beneath the moon and nobody cared about a thing.

And, before the rain came, we ran for the city limits. We took off through the trees and over mountaintops. We knew we'd be young forever. We knew we were the ones who made a difference.

We'll never stop. We'll keep pushing the boundaries. We'll keep pushing the limits of love until the day that we die.

Bleach, Blood & Cum

They look like kings. The men look so powerful and the women look so… so *owned.* I've fallen into this cycle of destruction… a chastity ring. That's what I like to call it. I've fallen into a miserable, lonely chastity ring, but I'm in love with it. I hate how lust can make us lethal. I love how it has. To be honest, I want to own your breath and sweat. I want to make you let it out, down your leg and onto the carpet. Whenever anyone asks me about my dreams, I lie. I tell them I want to be a doctor or lawyer. They all get really big smiles because they've seen my grades and know that I can get into those schools with the ivy growing on the side of the buildings.

I can't be honest with them. I don't even know how to explain it because there's no way that I can say it without sounding crazy. "I want the fame," I had told my friend once while drunk. He looked at me really funny and said, "The fame?" My mouth went dry and I shrugged. "I want to be a star, but the *other* kind. The kind you need an I.D. to see."

Go ahead. Laugh like he did. Just know that I had potential. Everyone always said that to me, but I didn't care. I never wanted to be a doctor or lawyer because they never had the type of power that I wanted. If you own someone sexually, you own everything about them. I want to run the world. I want to be your teenage fantasy. I want you to give in and use me for whatever you want. Let me be your wet dream. Touch yourself to me.

If you ever want to find me, I'll be in the far right corner of the bowling alley in Upper Macungie. I'll be drinking and throwing every game because that's how they like to play. It's amazing how we fall in love. It's amazing how happy I can be with something that makes me feel so oppressed and alone. The sickening yellow walls of that bowling alley feel so grungy and lonely, but I've gotten caught up in it. I've gotten caught up in the underground. There's this little camera that monitors all the lanes above the snack stand and I've fallen in love with kissing her in front of it and imagining someone watching it in fifty years and seeing me in black and white, laughing and marrying failure.

I just want to have it all. I remember the first time that I touched myself. It was mostly an accident how I had found the picture, but it made me feel really good. I let it all out and then felt really exposed and guilty about how something could completely and utterly control me. I loved the way they looked. Parts of their bodies made me really excited and I hadn't really realized it until then.

I wanted more. I wanted to do it. I wanted to own somebody the way they owned me. I wanted to make the videos. I wanted to be inside of them. My sister walked in on me once while I was doing it. I guess that's when it all began. It was just having *one* set of eyes that gave me the idea of glory.

That night was nothing like I'd ever imagined. It wasn't supposed to end the way that it did. She looked worn out, like a girl who was just *tired* of it all. I knew that she was older than me at the time because she wasn't even a senior anymore and I was only a freshman. We met outside the bowling alley when we were hotboxing in Josh's truck and seeing how long we could hold a lit cigarette to our wrists. She came to the window, scratching at it with her long, red nails and asking for a buck fifty so she could get a soda to mix with her Everclear. She'd smile at me and scratch my arms with her nails. She looked like one of the girls that I had saved on my computer. When we went inside, we bowled a few games and my friends left to smoke a bowl outside. I was alone with this girl; the one with the denim jacket, pink skirt and bleached curls that spilled from her head like rotini. Her face looked chalky and her lips looked too red for her pale face, or maybe it was just the fluorescents. She started blowing really big bubbles with her bubblegum and telling me that she was really bored. I said I was bored too and she took me to the girl's bathroom because there's a shitty lock on it. I started talking about how my friends were going to come back soon because I was nervous, but she started touching my chest really strangely and running her nails across my arms again. She had eye shadow that smeared all over my white t-shirt when we were kissing and touching each other. My body felt lustful, but my stomach just didn't feel right. There was something about her that made me feel inhuman. She felt cold, especially when she was naked and I could feel her bare skin. We'd just rub ourselves together and rub all the sweat and cum around until we couldn't breathe right anymore. She'd make noises while I did it. She'd claw at my shoulders and puncture the skin. I couldn't feel the sting because my legs were trembling and I was holding too much inside of me.

She reached a hand into my discarded jeans and pulled out my phone. She thrust it into my hands and told me to take her picture. She told me to take video of it all and I started clicking through my phone's menu with shaking fingers.

"Take my picture," she breathed. "Take my picture…"

I snapped a few shots before switching to video. I propped it against the faucet of the sink and kept rubbing myself against her. My back arched. My lips quivered. I let it go inside of her because I felt like I could do anything to her in front of that camera. There was such beauty in the destruction of it all. When I pulled out, I felt like I owned the night. I felt like I was living this teenage fantasy and grabbing a piece of "these happy days" and making them mine for everyone to see. I had the nail marks on my side to prove it. I had the bruise on my neck from her teeth and the brushed-burned kneecaps. When I was finished and the guilt that had been in my stomach started bubbling up, I fell backward into the puddle-filled tile. Pieces of paper towel and black hair clung to my palms. I pulled up my pants really quickly because I didn't know what else to do and then left the bathroom without washing my hands because I couldn't stand looking at her oily face anymore.

"Ya know," she called after me, crumpled like road kill across the wet floor, "you'll always remember what happened here. You'll never forget tonight." Her lips broke into a weak smile. "You did it, kid. You did it."

My lips start quivering again. My knees felt really sore and I first took notice to the fact that my gums were bleeding.

"You'll never forget me," she whispered, starting to cry, "I'll never fade away. You grew up today, kid. You grew up."

And I unlatched the lock and let the door slam behind me. I knew that she only let me inside of her because her boyfriend broke up with her the weekend before and her father always hit her across the cheek and called her a pig since she was little.

Sex is just sex. I'll never understand why it owns us, but it *fascinates* me how it does. I was so *owned* by that video every night before bed. I put it online one day and got off to people commenting on it and saying really sexual things. They'd talk about how degraded she looked and how much they loved it. I felt left out because nobody was talking about me, so I started taking pictures of myself naked and posting them on gay sites.

I'd become obsessed with being objectified because it was such an interesting brand. One time, when I was drinking with my friend, I took video of myself and him jacking off in front of the camera. The faceless men on the websites told me that they wanted to see me spit in his mouth and do other weird things. I did.

The baseball team got together one night at Ricky's house on the top of the hill. We drank a few cans of beer and tried to throw his cat into the fire until it ran away. I thought that night was going to be the greatest night of my life because the bonfire burnt so high and I remember feeling like I owned it. It was really warm beside that fire like it was warm inside of her. It was tight and warm inside that girl and I suddenly craved for that feeling again. There was a girl there that had a really nice smile. Her lips tasted sweet- nothing like the girl I had met outside the bowling alley. I had my letterman jacket on and she said that I looked so strong inside of it. She was nothing like the other girls. I mean, her blond hair fell across her shoulders like it does for the girls in the magazines. The way the fire sparkled in her eyes made her look so incredibly determined. She dragged me to my dad's old truck in Ricky's driveway. We kissed a lot and she started touching me down there. The beer gave me a nice buzz and warmed my blood as we smiled and made funny noises while touching. She didn't know what she was doing but we still laughed because she was so cute and funny inside her tight jeans and A&E sweater. I liked how she didn't know. It made me feel powerful.

We drove to the baseball diamond behind our high school while listening to *Journey* and *The Who*. We stumbled out of the car and I was surprised that the night didn't feel cold. She kept saying my name while we walked to home plate. I told her to take off her jeans and shirt and then I started feeling her chest because I wanted my hands to be as close to her heart as they could. My name sounded so beautiful when she said it. "James Davis." It sounded so unique when it slipped from her lips. She told me to imagine that the field lights were bathing us in gold. She told me to take her and imagine cheering from the broken stands like I was a legend. "You're something, Davis," she'd say. "You're something."

And I knew how to do it now- especially because I remembered what I had done to that broken girl in the bowling alley. I pulled it all off. We started kissing again beneath the swirling stars and I felt like one of them. "You're something, Davis. You're something…" And I knew I was. I kept feeling her chest. My knees were getting irritated from the gravel, but I couldn't feel the stinging because my legs were trembling and I wasn't afraid this time. Her lips were so tiny. They hugged mine and made them feel so loved. I pulled my phone from my jacket and began recording her and me as we started having sex.

With a rattling breath, she pulled back. I let my eyes peel open and then wander across her naked body. When my gaze reached her face, she looked really scared.

"James?" she asked me, worried. "James, what is that?"

I lowered the camera. My smile shifted sideways and I knew that she was going to be angry that I was recording us. She was going to make me delete the videos and then she was going to leave me on home plate, hard and alone.

"No," she said, "*that.*"

She didn't point, but I knew that she was talking about my body. I backed up and let my eyes travel down my stomach. At first, I didn't know what it was. After a few seconds, I realized that the small patch of red burned when I touched it.

"James?" she asked. "James, what is that, huh? What is that?"

And I'll always remember how embarrassed I was. I'll always remember how I threw my pants up to cover it. I'll always remember how ashamed, confused, and scared I was when the moonlight fell across that patch of red. It glistened just below my pubic bone, a simple brushstroke of red skin that looked almost like a tongue. As my heart sank and body went rigid, I was positive that things would never be the same again. I'd seen the movies in class. I'd seen it all.

It had been three whole years since that night in the bathroom and inside the bowling alley with the popcorn scent of rental shoes, shitty 80s music and broken crane game. You never think it'll come to you, but when it gets there, you can't fight it anymore. You think about this chastity ring and wonder how many people's blood you'll be thinking about the next time you let go. It's been three years since then and I've realized that all this blood and cum have become spoiled milk. They aren't any good anymore. They bubble up like toxins. They're just no good.

That was the first night that I couldn't stop crying. I drove home, sobbing with red, itchy eyes and chattering teeth. Ever since then, every time I tried to get off to porn, I couldn't. It'd take me forever and I'd start crying while thinking about how lonely those girls look in it. People may not realize it because they're too busy watching it all… but look into the girls' eyes. They look so broken, like they're being dehumanized and treated like broken, little dolls. They look so lonely and I can't get off thinking about how much they must hate themselves.

My cum looks like blood now. It looks so bloody and red when it comes out of me and into my hands. I let it fall between my fingers because it scares me so much to think about how my blood is poisoned because of sex. I fall back onto my bed and make the baseball posters fall from the wall. I scream because I'm bleeding from a place where nobody should be bleeding. When I turn on the lights, I realize that I'm just imagining everything and that I'm only bleeding because I ripped the scabs from my knuckles on the zipper of my jeans. With all of it cupped inside my hand, I stumble across the room and grab for the bleach beside my stained pads and socks. I pour it into my hands, cry, and pray that it'll clean me until I'm free of everything poisonous inside of me.

I let it all fall from my hands and onto my comforter. It happens every night. I've become obsessed with bleach, blood and cum. I've become obsessed with distilling the monster. I sit for hours, spilling myself into my hands and bleeding out because I want to get it all *out* of me. I want to feel pure again. I want to feel like that boy who owned the night on the baseball diamond because people would fantasize about *that* boy, not the venomous one whose sex is like a lethal injection.

The bleach burns. My skin feels so raw. I feel so cold. The blood and cum runs down the side of the blue, bleach bottle and mixes together and reminds me of the dream. I rub it all around. I just keep rubbing that sticky grease around until I see the red, white and blue and dream about how I could've had it all and I could've been perfect.

What am I now? A chastity monster. I wear a chastity ring because it makes me feel so innocent and girls like them. When I taint it with the nasty flow, I feel so destructive. I sit there for *hours*, touching myself and spilling myself until I'm raw and aching. Sometimes, I do live-streams on those shitty websites that old men go on to masturbate. They say really sexual things to me and I never see their faces. A million miles separate us and I get this feeling… this feeling that I could be their everything. When I finally fall asleep, I dream about living infinitely in shitty moments and low-budget pornos. I wake up, shout, and start ripping the posters from the wall. I smash the baseball bat against the plaster and knock each blade from the ceiling fan because I'm so gone. The golden boys on the stand break off really easily, and their bent arms speckle the floor like lost spider legs. I pour the bleach onto the bed and watch it spill over onto the carpet because I just want to be someone's teenage fantasy. Nobody wants to be mine though. I've become something so used and discarded and I'll only be able to find love with the equally broken.

I watch the old videos from my phone of when I had sex with that beaten-down girl in the bathroom and I get really angry. Her grunts and moans pervade the room and her voice rips at my ears. *"Take my picture. Don't forget me. Never forget me."*

The music makes me uncomfortable now- that creepy music that plays in the background during the pornos. It makes me feel like I can do anything and that I can own the nights again in a different way. A wave of guilt, lust, and fury rolls over me and I start crying again because I'm so consumed with the quest for sexual fame because it's all I can ever do now.

One night, I grabbed the keys to my truck and pulled onto route 222. I still had blood on my hands and I wasn't wearing a lot of clothing. My breath was fogging the windshield and the blood flakes fell to my lap like eraser shavings.

I pulled into the parking lot around eleven o'clock and stumbled out of the car. Everything looked familiar, from the vending machine to the tire mark on the sidewalk before the door. The ashtray was littered with cigarette butts and someone had vomited down its side.

I knew that she'd be there. I knew because she's *always* there. Every Friday night, she's at the bowling alley, standing outside smoking and mixing her diet cola with her Everclear. Her curls are much shorter now and she has a piercing that looks like a sparkling mole above her lip. Her face muscles look weaker now, like they've given up on holding her face in place. She looks late 30s, much older than I thought she was back when we rubbed together and breathed heavily. When she saw me, her red eyes grew even larger and an elated breath escaped her lips.

"I *knew*," she breathed, "I *knew....*"

"You..." I shouted. "It was you, you did it!"

She dropped the cigarette to the pavement and smeared it with her heel. "I... I told you. I told you that you'd always remember me."

Tears of frustration leaked from the corner of my eyes. "You gave me... you gave me..."

Three years had gone by. The bowling alley was still the same shitty place it was before. The heart was still probably scribbled across the stall inside the bathroom and the glory hole probably still waited in the men's bathroom for some warmth. Everything was timeless and the same. Everything but me. I was just as broken and used as this place and I never was like that before.

"You gave me... gave me *AIDS.*"

She started crying too. "Don't you understand? Don't you see?"

I kept choking on my tears. My eyes fluttered back and forth and I couldn't see what she meant. "I'm gonna die. You know that, right? I'm gonna... I'm gonna..."

She spread out her arms. "This is my *Hollywood.*"

And, at that moment, I finally understood. I finally understood what was broken about the world. Despite the fact that I hated her, I couldn't stop myself from pulling her into a hug and crying with her as it rained on us outside of that hell-hole with the bright, neon lights and empty arcade.

"My name's Marilyn," she wept into my sleeve. "Nobody ever cares about learning my name. And this... this is my stardom. Take my picture. Please, just take my picture."

My phone felt heavy inside my pocket. My face was slicked with rainwater and the blood and cum began dripping from my fingers and running down my leg.

"We'll be something, James. This can be our Hollywood. This can be our stardom."

Brutus: Part One

Bruce Farrel is everything. He's everything I've ever dreamed of being. During those chilly nights, I'd watch him beneath those silver lights. He'd be amazing- he really would. The way he ran down the field was beautiful. The thundering of his cleats would sound like music to me. He didn't run on the grass like the others. No, he wasn't anything like the others. Bruce Farrel ran on piano keys.

He's everything to everyone, but he doesn't wear a crown, he wears a football helmet. He isn't a king, he's a captain. He isn't a God, he's a hometown hero.

Bruce Farrel has a lot of girlfriends. Well, not the way you think. I mean, it's not like he's *fucking* them or anything. No, Bruce Farrel isn't like that. He'd never do that. I mean, it's not like he can't. No, don't get me wrong. He really *can*. He just doesn't want to. Nope, that's not Bruce Farrel. Bruce isn't like that at all. He could be though. He really could be like that and nobody would care. I mean… he's Bruce *Farrel*. He can be whatever he wants to be.

He's a legend. He's everything anyone ever wanted to be. He drives a nice car- a really nice one. He always has people around his locker. When he broke his ankle during football doubles last year, everyone offered to carry his books around for him when he was on crutches. I wanted to offer, but I knew the other boys would laugh at me.

There's something about his smile. There's something awfully *addictive* about the way that kid laughs- even if it's fake. There's something about how stupid he is that makes him look like he knows what the hell he's talking about. Actually, he is smart. I didn't mean that he's retarded or anything. He just isn't the greatest at algebra. But honestly, who cares about algebra anyway? Bruce Farrel makes algebra look lame. He makes it look all faggy. He makes me hate everything about Algebra.

But why am I so goddamn *good* at it?

I used to be his friend way back when. Well, I tutored him in ninth grade. He said I was funny. He told me that I was smart. Maybe… just maybe for a microscopic moment, an *ounce* of a second, Bruce Farrel wanted to be like me. Maybe, just maybe, he looked at me with awe for once.

I want to be Bruce Farrel. Heck, sometimes I even want to *date* Bruce Farrel. But not like that. I'm not a queerbag. I hate it when people say that about me. I know me. Other people don't. I'm not a fag. I'm not gay. I'm not some homo. But God, there's something about Bruce Fucking Farrel. He has such a nice smile. Jesus Christ, why the fuck does he have such a nice smile?

Bruce Farrel is everything. Everyone talks about him all the time. He's quite a "hip" thing to talk about. Sometimes, if you talk about him long enough, you feel like he's your friend. But he's not. No, Bruce Farrel would never be friends with someone like me. The rejection is what makes him cool.

He's cool. Everything about him is cool. Sometimes when I'm around him, I pretend like I'm cool too. I want him to think I'm cool. I can be cool.

I can be cool.

Our junior year schedules smelled like coffee when we got them on September sixth. That's probably what that brown splatter on Kelly Watson's was. Tutoring forms were sent out by the librarian. She has this really annoying handwriting and always dots her "i's" like Walt Disney. This year though, there were no annoying "i's" on my paper. No, hell no. None.

I'm tutoring Bruce Farrel in College Algebra. I've never tutored a senior before. He's pretty bad at it. He doesn't know how to add integers correctly or multiply with negatives and positives. And don't even get me started on cat-and-whisker-plots…. But there's still something about his confused expression that makes him look like a cool kid. He wears this really smelly cologne from one of those stores in the mall. But it's not like I sit there and fucking *smell* him. No, that would be creepy. I don't bury my nose in his shirt or anything. I just waft. I waft the scent like we were taught in Biology.

I waft the scent of Bruce Farrel.

He's still everything. He's not quite so much *everything* anymore. Not as much as he was last year. It was like he could tell though. He used to be everyone's everything. He used to make sense. He's still amazing on the field. He can throw like he was born to be a football player. He's still captain. His head is still heavy with the football helmet. Everyone still loves him. He still sucks at math. He still wins all the home games. His name bleeds all over the newspapers. It's like he's a movie star.

Sometimes, I wonder what it would be like. I wonder what it would be like to be a hometown hero. It must be something. I'd love the cheers. I'd love all those girls cheering for me. I'd love to be able to go to the parties and *fuck* all the girls that I wanted. Even when Bruce Farrel calls me names or pushes me against a locker, I still *wish* I could be an ounce of that hometown hero.

CP English classes read <u>Julius Caesar</u> during first semester of senior year. I read that during freshman year because I was in advanced.

Bruce Farrel doesn't understand it.

"I don't get what the dude says in it. I don't get what's so *bad* about the Ides of March. I don't even know who the fuck *Brutus* is."

I un-bent the corner of the page that he was reading. Honestly, I *hate it* when people bend the pages of their books. "Brutus is Caesar's friend, but then he betrays him in the end."

"Sounds like a douche."

I nodded. "Yeah, but it wasn't all Brutus's fault. A group of aristocrats convinced him to do it."

"Aristocrats?"

"Never mind that. Just remember that Brutus killed Caesar on the Ides of March."

I could see his brain cranking somewhere inside his pretty little head. He nodded, but I could tell it was robotic, like he didn't actually realize he was doing it.

I was satisfied with his shallow nod. I couldn't be a nerd. No, not around Bruce Farrel. I had to be his reflection. Maybe then, he'd invite me to those parties. Maybe then, I'd be a cool kid.

As days continued, something changed in him. He lost his big head altogether. There wasn't even a trace of the damn thing. People started to notice the differences. He didn't talk about fucking girls all the time, and as an eleventh grade boy, that was a target. He didn't *use* girls. He didn't *degrade* girls. He didn't *make fun* of the weaker. He didn't *fight* other guys. He didn't *punch* other guys.

But rumor had it… rumor had it that he *kissed* another guy at some crazy party with the "jocks and cheerleaders."

But I didn't believe it. I couldn't believe it. He was Bruce Farrel. He didn't do that. He couldn't be insecure. He couldn't be broken. No, that'd ruin him. He couldn't be weak. Not that kissing another guy made him weak. That's not what I meant. I just meant that… he wasn't as golden as he was before. I wished it wasn't true. I didn't want him to be a faggot. No, that would *ruin* it. That'd make me *not* want to be his friend. Nothing was redeeming about the kid if he suddenly didn't have it all.

The rumor was proven false. I didn't believe it. Nobody believed it. But Bruce Farrel hoped that we did. He even convinced himself that we did. He knew, deep down, that we all knew. But he never said anything. He ate lunch with the football boys. He started talking about fucking girls. He looked down girl's shirts all of a sudden and started calling other people fags and dykes.

And I still tutored him in math and English every Wednesday.

But he didn't act around me. He never pretended to be that golden boy that he used to be when I was around. There was something…. something *timeless* about the little piece of hellish high school that we had the blessed fortune of sharing together. He could tell I despised the place. And honestly, he could tell that I knew *he* despised the place too.

I wanted to be his best friend. I admired the way he could make other people look at him. Teachers always loved the hell out of the kid. They showered him with praise and other classmates were lucky if they get a few sprinkles of compliments every so often. Maybe his coolness could rub off on me? Maybe if I hung around the kid, I could be someone else's Bruce Farrel.

I know I can.

I started tutoring him at his house. It smelled like Febreze. Actually, it kind of smelled like him. He still sucked at fractions. He stared down at the blank paper and crinkled his forehead together, like the answers would come with psychic energy.

He was dumb. He was stupid. He was going *nowhere* in life.

But he was cool. And I felt like I was his best friend.

And we'd start talking about more than just trivial math problems. We'd start talking about his day. We'd talk about football practice. We'd talk about stupid cheerleaders and the kid who threw up in the hallway.

We'd laugh a lot. And it was nice, for once, to know that I had a friend.

That's right, I had a *friend.*

For the first time in my fucking pathetic life, I had someone to talk to… someone who hadn't given birth to me. I had a friend.

I didn't lust for Bruce Farrel. No, not at all. There was not a fiber in my body that was attracted to him. But for some reason…I was in love with him. I was in love with Bruce Farrel.

Bruce Farrel was one lonely kid. I thought he had it all, but when I talked to him, I realized Bruce Farrel wasn't anything. He was just a little boy. He was insecure. He was afraid. He was dumb. He was going through the motions.

We got drunk a few times and talked. He'd wear his football jersey a lot around me. He got a girlfriend named Jenna. She was pretty. She had this long, golden blonde hair that she braided to the side. She was a cheerleader.

Bruce would tell me about how he fucked her. And I don't know why, but I'd be disappointed. I'd be disappointed that someone mattered to him more than I did.

I didn't want to fuck him or anything, but I was in love with everything about him. And even though he had a girlfriend, I'm sure he was in love with me too.

One night, things broke apart. Things broke apart around us… the kids of the suburbs. I thought we were going to make it. Hell, when I saw Bruce Farrel on that football field, I thought we already *did* make it. There was no doubt in my mind, the night of that football game, that the kids of the suburbs had graduated from their insecurities.

I cheered for him. I know I shouldn't have, but I felt confident that I had someone like him to back me up. I cheered for him when he made that touchdown and people started talking. They talked because I only cheered for him. They talked because I'd only ever gone to a football game once or twice before. They talked because I always sat in the back row, never the front. They talked because I used his *first* name. They started making something out of nothing. The kids… the ones with the sideways smirks asked me if I was his boyfriend. They laughed at me and started calling him a fag.

It was like a battle cry. I thought the war was over. I thought we *made it.* But that cry led to another- one that didn't signal victory.

Why? Why are they so cruel?

I pray for the kids in the suburbs. I pray that one day, we'll all graduate from similarity. They're so cruel. The kids of the suburbs can be so cruel.

Why are they so cruel?

I thought I could be someone. I wanted a piece of that hometown hero.

I could be cool.

I am cool.

But still, those kids are so damn cruel.

And I saw Bruce Farrel turn around on the field, with his sweating face and legendary stare. He gave us all a look from the field- a look of utter bewilderment.

And it confused me, because he looked at me then. He looked at me, and gave me a look of confusion too. He didn't look happy to see me. He looked... frustrated.

I felt like a nag. Why did I feel like such a fucking nag?

He looked so glorious in that football uniform- just like the gladiators looked with their helmets and armor. He looked, in this one frame of time, like a timeless hero that'd never fall. And even though the high school football games were wrapping up, and he'd *never* be on this field again, I still couldn't imagine a world that wasn't run by people like Bruce Farrel.

He told me to wait for him after the game. He told me to wait for him beneath the bleachers. I couldn't tell if he was in a good or bad mood, because he often looked caught between two emotions. But tonight, he seemed angry with me, but also amused. He seemed afraid of me, but also in control.

So I waited in the darkness beneath the bleachers. The pounding of feet faded to silence. The moon rose higher and higher in the chilly sky. The silver lights of the football stadium blinked to darkness.

And I was there, alone, for what seemed to be forever. Loose pieces of trash and gum wrappers were blowing across the grimy concrete. Fallen hats, bags and shoelaces littered the floor. There was even a broken doll in a puddle- one of those knockoff Barbie dolls made in Japan or something. Her arm said her name was GLORIA.

As more and more time clocked by, I began feeling angry. I was angry that I had wasted my night, waiting in the darkness beneath the bleachers. I was *angry* that Bruce Farrel was so ashamed of admitting to other people that he was my friend. I was angry at the suburbs. I was angry at how *easily* people can discard things.

But I heard footsteps approaching. There were a lot of them- meaning that Bruce Farrel wasn't alone. My heart perked.

Did Bruce Farrel finally tell his friends? Did he finally… did he finally think I was *cool*?

I knew I could be cool.

I was cool.

They were laughing. They still had their football uniforms on. A few of them looked drunk. There were cheerleaders with two of them. The kid with the buzzed hair was smoking a cigarette. Bruce Farrel was in the middle, with his wavy brown hair. As he stopped in front of me, I was too afraid to open my mouth.

"You waited?" he asked. He seemed happy, but I couldn't read him very well. The moonlight wasn't slanting across his face.

I took a timid step forward. My eyes swept across the jocks and cheerleaders. My body began growing hot. I felt nervous. I felt embarrassed.

"Yeah," I mumbled. "Just like you said."

Bruce Farrel started laughing- one of those addicting laughs. His other friends laughed too. They were low and nasally.

"Why are you following me around all the time?" Bruce asked me. "Why'd you come tonight, huh? Why'd you come?"

My heart sank a little, because I realized he was going to put on a show. I realized he needed to. I understood.

I shrugged. "I… I dunno."

He wasn't satisfied. He asked me again. The jocks and cheerleaders kept laughing. I was getting angry… angry that he didn't just *stop* right then. I was playing along. Couldn't that be enough?

But Bruce Farrel walked forward, stopping inches from my face. I didn't know what he was going to do, so I took a step back into the metal poles of the bleachers.

The others couldn't hear what he was saying to me anymore. They started talking amongst themselves. And it was incredibly unbelievable that they were so… so calm in this environment.

The kids of the suburbs are so cruel. How could *anybody* ever feel comfortable?

"Why you followin' me around? Huh? Why are you always there, watching me and trying to... to *talk* to me? You like me? Is that it? You got a crush on me or something?"

I was too caught off guard to answer.

"*Well?*" he prompted.

"Don't... don't you know?" I stammered.

"Tell me."

And that's when I picked up on the curiosity in his voice... the *real* curiosity in his voice.

I dropped my voice low, so nobody could hear. "Because Bruce, you're my *friend*. We hang out when nobody's around. We have *fun*. We talk about things and we... we... I don't know, we *understand* each other."

My voice cracked to silence. I slunk back a little bit further. My shoes nearly slid on the stones beneath me.

I was waiting for Bruce to smile. I was waiting for that chiseled face to break into a grin. But that never happened. He just looked at me, confused. That's when I realized he *wasn't* acting.

"You're my.... my fucking *tutor*. That's it. You're my tutor."

Bruce Farrel wasn't lying to me. He wasn't acting. I knew he wasn't. I forgot that he *never* acted around me. He was serious. I was mistaken. I was dumb, stupid, naïve. Bruce Farrel would never be friends with someone like me. I felt stupid. I felt like a stupid nerd waiting for the pretty boy beneath the bleachers.

One of the jocks piped up behind us. He whipped something over his head. It hit my shoulder and I cried in pain.

He had thrown a stone.

The kids laughed. The cheerleaders giggled and slapped their boyfriend's hands. "*Stop,*" they laughed, "that's mean. Don't be so mean."

But they said it in that voice. They smiled while they said it, like they secretly loved the alpha-male inside their boyfriends and jocks.

That's how we are in the suburbs. We're the kids… the kids of the suburbs.

The other football boys grabbed stones too. They threw them at me. I cried as they collided with my knee, shin, shoulder, chest, neck.

They kept laughing while they did it.

"*Let's stone the fag!*" one of the drunk boys shouted. "Let's *stone* him!"

So they did.

Suddenly, I was bleeding everywhere. There were bruises that had already turned yellow after only a few minutes. There were cuts and scrapes. The stones kept smashing against my head and face. I'd wince. I'd put bruised arms up in order to keep them from blackening my eyes.

The girls joined in too. Everyone threw stones. Everyone. Even Bruce Fucking Farrel.

He laughed louder than the others. He threw the biggest ones too. He kept calling me a fag while he did it. He kept aiming for my eyes.

He stoned me that night. He laughed at me. He fell into the constant motion of *similarity*.

After nearly fifteen minutes, I was curled up on the rocky ground. I couldn't see the moon anymore. My lungs felt popped. My nose was bleeding into my swollen mouth. I knew I was going to die.

The entire pack of jocks and cheerleaders seemed shocked… shocked at what they had done. But they stood firm. They kept their letterman jackets on and complained about being cold. They said they wanted to ditch me.

But Bruce Farrel knew I was going to die. His breath rattled in front of him. He let the remaining handful of stones fall to the ground like rain. "Is he dead? Did we kill him?"

"He's still shaking."

Bruce turned to face his friends. "Let's go then. We can go to the lake or something. We can drink up at the lake."

I tried to turn over. My loud groan echoed beneath the bleachers.

"Aw, someone put him out," one of the drunken cheerleaders whined. "He looks so… so broken."

I suddenly felt hands on my back. Pain was sent shooting down my arms and legs from the simple touch. My skin felt like tenderized hamburger.

The small slits of my eyes flickered over to Bruce Farrel, who was kneeling beside my crumpled masses. I smelled alcohol on his breath. He no longer held stones. He held a pocket knife.

And I knew he wasn't having fun anymore. He looked like he was going to vomit at the hands of what he created. He was dazed, but *aware*. He knelt beside me with that blade because he didn't know how else to stop it.

But you can't kill the suburbs with a blade. You can't stab it. You can't make it bleed.

My broken lips peeled open. "I thought… I thought you were my… my *friend*. They've killed me."

He didn't say anything. He seemed suddenly hit by a wave of realization.

My eyes met the knife. "You have a knife. You're killing me. You too..."

Tears glided down his cheeks. They smeared the black paint beneath his eyes.

"You too? You too… Bru-"

My voice faded to silence again. I was just about to whisper his name, but I stopped myself. I wanted to be Bruce Farrel's everything. I wanted him to *remember* me.

"*Brutus?*"

It was terribly haunting- it really was.

He returned the blade to his pocket and ran. He left me there to stand before the gateway to death. He left me there to bleed and attract ants and flies. He left me lying in a puddle like a broken doll.

I could hear his car peeling out of the parking lot. The kids were probably inside that nice convertible, laughing and drinking. They were headed to the lake, then their boxy little homes on hilltops. They were beautiful people. They were flawless. They were glorious. And I wondered, before I died, if they finally thought I was cool.

I could be cool.

I could be cool.

I had to forgive him. I had to forgive what he did to me. He killed me, but I couldn't hold it against him. He needed forgiveness. He was Brutus. He was Brutus and he needed to be forgiven. He was glorious. He was Brutus… Brutus *Farrel*.

Suburbia

My name is J. Merridew. I had a dream once. The walls of the house were stained with black muck and the floor was flooded with a thin stream of piss, vomit and beer. I was so worried because my new white shoes were going to get dirty and they were really expensive. My eardrums were ringing beneath the sledgehammer beats of house music. There were kids all around me- some wearing plain white tees and others wearing nothing at all. Their smiles were so white in that black blur, just like their shirts. They all knew who I was. They all knew my name. They took pictures with me and smiled at me from across the steaming bodies that were cramming together on the dance floor. I was somebody in that dream. I was important and loved.

I woke up. I wasn't sad, I was just angry. I was *angry* because I knew that it wasn't true. That night, I wanted to cry because I dreamed about how these kids finally thought that I was cool and I realized that's all I've ever wanted.

When I'd look in my bedroom mirror last year, I'd always see a black silhouette that was weak. My stomach would clench and my lips would fall into a heavy frown. My arms weren't big (and still aren't). My abs weren't chiseled like the statues I saw in Rome (and still aren't). I was nothing like the other boys with the high black socks and letterman's jackets. That's all I'd ever wanted. I just wanted to be like all the other boys. I wanted to follow them into the locker room because it must've felt great to live the life of a hometown hero. There was something so... so *appealing* about the confetti and loudspeakers. I wanted to own the suburban streets and make out with the girls beneath the bleachers.

I never used to care. Back during senior year, I used to drink before the football games and have my friends drive me to the stadium. I'd never watch the game because I was far too preoccupied with the lights, hotdogs, and shitty scoreboard. My friends and I would slur our words together and pretend to be something. We'd put on our leather jackets, dangle a bottle of rum in our hands, and swoon over our futures like we knew what was coming. I was content back then. I was living my ignorant existence in my equally ignorant world.

I grew up one day. That night was lonely- the night with too much cloud cover, a bit of wind, and obnoxious swarms of moths around the porch lights. My ears buzzed. My eyes soaked up the smiles that suddenly looked so sinister. It was then that I realized that these people suddenly looked like deadbeats. They looked so hopeless but I couldn't stop feeling like a joke to them. To this very day, I still feel like people are laughing at me. It's probably just me being crazy, but I can never tell. People used to make fun of me. They used to laugh at me in the hallway and I swore to myself that they would never do it again. I started noticing how much I hated being different in the suburbs. I started noticing how much I wanted to throw away originality to fall into a constant motion of similarity. I just wanted people to look at me like I was something. I just wanted people to think I wasn't a loser. They never made fun of me after I started dressing like them. When I looked like them and acted like them, they started to like me.

Can you blame me? I was born in the suburbs. It's so hard to break out of the white picket fence.

There was this boy. He played football. He had brown hair that was short and reminded me of the men in the Marines. His name wasn't Bruce Farrel, but he reminds me a lot of him. He was nominated for homecoming king. I'd never even heard of him until the loudspeaker belched out his name and number. After that night, I started noticing him in the hallways. *He* was built. *He* had big arms. *His* abs looked like the statues I saw in Rome.

And there was something about him. Something about *him* that made me hate *myself.* I just wanted to be him. I looked up to him all of a sudden and never wanted to wear my leather jacket again. After that, he was everything that I wanted to be. And it was terribly strange. High school was wrapping up. The football team was handing in their jerseys. He was going absolutely *nowhere* in life, but I couldn't imagine a world not run by people like him.

He was everything. He was everything I'd ever dreamed of being. He wasn't fictitious, but I made him out to be. I made him into one of those little superstars that everyone wants to get to know but nobody can.

To this very day, a small, screwed-up part of me still wants to be him. I see him when I go back to my hometown, and I still admire how he can make people look at him. I admire how he did everything right to be this little trophy boy who I hated in high school because I always envied him. He was everything. Everyone talked about him all the time. He was cool. Everything about him was cool. Sometimes when I was around him, I pretended like I was cool too. I wanted him to think I was cool. I could be cool.

I could be cool.

Still, I try to be cool.

I never used to wear the high black socks. I never used to have those douchebag ear piercings, the diamond studs that make me look like such a tool. I never used to be so obsessed with fitting in. In a way, it's embarrassing. Becoming a cardboard cutout is like shooting individuality in the face. But I can't help it. I just want to belong. Don't we all? Don't we all just want to be that hometown hero? It's so difficult to be different in such a similar environment. It molded me into a figure who embraced similarity in order to fit in. Look at me now. Can't you tell? Can't you tell that my life was once infinitely devoted to not standing out or causing waves? I still get that feeling sometimes that people are laughing at me and I can't handle it. Maybe there's something different about me. Nobody admires these boys anymore except for me. Nobody cares about the stupid jocks in high school that went to community college and studied business. There was just something about how they were admired that makes me admire them to this very day.

I just want to be admired. I just want *them* to think that *I'm* cool for once. I just look back and realize how many kids fall into the constant motion of similarity because we all just want to belong. I just want to be perfect. I'm a perfectionist in every way but I'll never be happy with it all because there's always someone better out there.

Every year when I was younger, I'd sit in my plastic dollhouse and stare out the window at the firework display that would rain out above the evergreen trees in my yard. The fair would be a mile or two outside the neighborhood. On the last night of the fair, hundreds of fireworks would explode in the sky and my Mom would always watch them with my brother and me. It would be eleven o'clock at night. I'd be lucky if I didn't fall asleep by then. The grand finale would shake our house because we'd be so close. Wisps of smoke would dance through the starry sky and I'd dream about how I wanted to grow up and live with my family in a beautiful house overlooking beautiful blue and green fireworks.

I'd dream a lot as a kid- especially while I watched those fireworks bursting over suburbia.

I never want to dream about that again. I love my parents, but I'd rather wander down the shitty alleyways and marry failure than jog the suburban streets and marry similarity. When I die, I want to be buried in my leather jacket instead of a suit and tie. I've always hated ties.

Pray for us. Pray for the kids of the suburbs. Pray that one day, we'll graduate from similarity. I tried to be cool. I was cool. But still, those kids were so damn cruel. Why were they so cruel? Why was it so hard to break free from being a loser?

I was such a loser back then. I'll never be like that again. I'll become my own hometown hero. I'll prove everyone wrong. I still see the stadium lights when I go home on Fridays in early October. I remember how part of me was created by the desire to be somebody back then. It's funny. It really is. Now, I look at all these boys and understand why they wear the same thing and talk the same way and like the same things.

They're just a product of their boxy little houses on hilltops. They haven't realized it yet. They haven't realized that they can throw paint on the white picket fence, burn down the conformity and kill the suburbs.

And so it begins.

I have a lot of anger that has turned into sadness. It's about time that I expose our suburban icons for what they really are.

Because boys who have it all always lose it all.

And when they do, they fall from their pretty, little havens. Stars are only beautiful when they're above us. But when they fall from the sky, oh, that's such a sight to see.

The more I wanted to be Bruce, the more I hated myself. It's time that the stars come crashing down. It's time that we wet the posters and magazines with ink and blood. It's time that the statues lose their sculpted heads and fall to rubble.

Turn the page.

Kill the idol.

Solo Cups & Bruises: Part Two

I brought a hand to the fresh scratches and red marks on my
neck. For a moment, I wondered why I'd done it. When I couldn't
come up with an answer, I wondered how many people bleed
because they want to, not because they have to.

It was warm inside my letterman jacket. I told myself that I
was never going to take it off. The only sounds that I could hear
were the whistling of the wind and the twisting of the chain swings.
The sky was beautiful that night. There were only stars, no clouds,
and I could see them really well because nobody had their porch
lights on anymore. The houses around me were just as still as the sky
and everything felt so eternal and never ending. I love when things
feel that way.

My hands were buried inside my pockets and I was singing a
really happy song because I was happy and I thought that it was
going to last forever. My fingertips were moist and kept sticking to
the soft baggie of purple pills inside my pocket—the only thing that I
had brought with me when I left my house that night. My father

hadn't known I'd left. He squeezed my shoulder and said goodnight before climbing the stairs to an empty bedroom.

I spent hours lying on that roundabout of that playground and singing and smiling and taking my pretty, purple pills. I'd squeeze them between two fingers and hold them up to the moon and say, "These pills look just like *pearls*. Pretty, purple pearls that are all for me."

Then, I'd swallow them and laugh some more and tell myself that I was happy. Afterward, I stood up from the roundabout and swung on the swings. I scratched away the upside down crosses that the other kids wrote on the slides and seesaw. I left the playground and started walking around the neighborhood, all the while, talking to myself like I had company. I pretended that I was walking my dog and would occasionally scoff at it for chasing imaginary cars. I imagined a woman beside me, one who loved me and had a beautiful ring on her finger. I pictured her kissing me all over my cheek and telling me that we've made it and that we're going to be okay.

Because, in reality, all I really wanted were things to be okay.

I was young that night and I was a dreamer. And things were all right for us. Things were okay because we all would walk around our pretty, suburban neighborhoods and take pills and laugh and smoke behind our sheds and no bad feelings ever scared us from behind because none of us were going anywhere anytime soon.

If I could, I'd live infinitely in that moment when I was lying on the playground and my biggest worry was the fact that I'd have to grow up someday. But that day, I told myself, was never going to come because I was wearing a letterman jacket that still fit and I was 18 years old and the scoreboard at the stadium was still new and the bleachers weren't rusted like they are now and the confetti had just rained down and people were young, dumb and hormonal and it didn't matter to me then that I wasn't your world because you weren't mine either.

Those pearls are so pretty. Pretty, purple pearls. All for me.

I stopped walking at the intersection of East View and Dumpling and traced the distant outlines of three beautiful houses. Tall trees defended their faces and the pools in their backyards were luxurious, little moats. They had oak front doors and porch lights that cascaded across perfectly manicured lawns that never seemed to grow. When I was younger, I always wanted to explore those yards. I wanted to trip over the sweating hoses in the summertime, but I never really knew why.

I puffed on a cigarette while leaning against the stop sign on the corner. I was never any good at blowing rings, but I busied myself for several minutes with that while I waited for the car to pull onto the road and blind me with its headlights.

I knew that he was going to be wearing his letterman jacket with his varsity letter ironed onto the back. He earned it. I bought mine at some vintage shop in the city, but I didn't care that I hadn't been handed mine on a stage with glistening gold and school officials with really shitty stage presence. To be honest, I didn't want to be like him the way that I used to. I wanted to cut off the sleeves of those expensive polos that I bought from the rich-kid stores in the mall and wear them to the fancy dinner parties my parents used to go to. I wanted people to look at me and think I was a degenerate, young kid with an attitude because... well....

At least they were looking at me.

I wanted to reject it all because I was sick of being perfect. I was so bored with normality and dreams of poster boys and tabloid covers.

But then, I realized the answer.

I kept puffing on that cigarette at that street intersection and staring at those beautiful houses that all looked the same and I said to myself, "It's not about leaving the suburbs. It's about making them good for me."

And I pumped my fist into the air in triumph as I laughed and grabbed hold of the stop sign before shielding my eyes from the car turning onto the road.

For a moment, I thought it was going to plow over the neighbor's mailbox. I smeared my cigarette on the street with the bottom of my hi-tops and leapt into the grass. Bruce was drunk—drunker than he should have been. The passenger window was rolled down and he was hollering something that I couldn't hear because his music was too loud.

"Bruce," I exhaled. "Get out of the car. I'm driving."

There was another shout—this time from a girl. I peered through the window and saw a cheerleader spread eagle in the back seat. She was twirling a ribbon between her fingers, the kind that the cheerleaders wear in their hair during football games. Her nails were painted real pretty and red. The polish was chipping near the tips and I could see some dirt beneath the small crescent-shaped nail on her pinky.

"Great," I murmured, "you brought a friend."

My eyes flickered over to Bruce, who was smiling at me with that guilty smile that he was famous for. "Ya know…" he breathed, "ya know I had to do it."

He lumbered out of the car and then gave me a big hug. My back cracked really loudly and I couldn't breathe very well. "Alright," I wheezed. "I get it, Bruce."

"Ya know," he whispered, "you're alright."

He released me. I flattened out the front of my jacket and nodded. I tried to smile because I didn't want him to think that I was annoyed that he had called me. My lips refused to curl. My high was almost gone.

"No matter what anyone says about you," he continued, "you're alright." And he poked my chest really hard with his finger, leaving some dirt on the third button of my jacket.

My eyes traced the small smudge and I snorted. "What does everyone say about me?"

He opened his mouth to speak, but then realized that he had said too much. In awkward response, he grunted, "I gotta piss," and wobbled from the street into the neighbor's yard.

There was a sudden rustle from the backseat, followed with a shout. "Bruce! Bruce, where are you going?"

"Calm down. He'll be back."

The girl laughed really hard again and started putting the ribbon on her upper lip and telling me that it was a mustache. I told her to go to sleep because Santa was coming.

When my eyes glided over her pathetic figure, they narrowed in curiosity. There was a heap of black on the backseat that I hadn't noticed before, tucked between her and the opposite door. She was resting her grubby feet on it and getting it really dirty. I needed to crane my neck through the window in order to make out what it was.

"What is that?"

"What's what?"

"That… that *thing* beside you."

The girl's eyes swept over top of it too and she smiled. "Oh, *that*. Bruce said it's a secret. It's *our* little secret…"

I shot a glance at Bruce's back. "But what is it?"

"It's a suitcase."

"A *suitcase*? Why do you guys have a suitcase?"

"Because," she began, "Bruce says we're going to run off together."

"Run off together?"

She nodded and started giggling through cupped hands. "He picked me up after the game tonight. At first, he wasn't right. He was really sad and I kissed him and then he told me that he wasn't sad anymore. He took me to his house and we packed a suitcase and got money for a motel. Bruce says that he wants to go someplace where they'll take his picture and put him on magazine covers."

"Magazine covers?"

"Yeah… he wants to sell a magazine like he's… like he's *Jimmy Dean*."

I nodded half-heartedly. At the time, I didn't realize that she wasn't kidding and that the suitcase was packed and ready. I didn't realize that if I had *looked* inside that suitcase I would have found nothing but broken football trophies and rusting plaques. Heaps of them. Ribbons and medals and fake gold. But beneath all the gold, I would've found something much more terrifying.

And I would've known in that moment if I had just bothered to look, but I ignored it all.

Bruce was peeing for a really long time and I just wanted to get things over with. After several moments spent listening to crickets, I shot a glance over toward his barrel-chested silhouette and realized that he was spelling his name on the neighbor's drive way.

"Bruce!" I scolded, "Stop that!"

Laughter again. It was such a gloating laughter. It sounded so stereotypically jock that my mood tanked a bit more.

Bruce trudged through a few low-cut shrubs with his muddy hi-tops. His zipper was open and a small patch of his yellow boxers spilled from the opening like pus from a wound.

"What were you doing before?" I asked as he rounded the car. "Were you drinking up at the lake?"

He nodded.

"How much?"

He held up seven fingers.

"You're an idiot," I spat.

He brushed shoulders with me in a playful way before laughing and getting into the passenger's seat. "What were you doing tonight?" he asked me. "Jacking off? I called you two hours ago. I know you weren't with anybody."

"I was walking around the neighborhood and smoking."

He laughed. "Well your night's about to get good."

"Oh yes," I said, my voice rich with sarcasm. "I'm sure it's going to be *golden*."

The thought of heading over to some girl's house and partying with all the field hockey girls who stuff their bras and take off their clothes after drinking watered-down vodka made me want to stick my tongue inside a mousetrap. Bruce didn't notice that I was making fun of him and continued to solidify my suspicions that his brain was filled with nothing more than memories of cheap porn and hot wings.

"Nice jacket," he smiled, prying me from my thoughts. He grabbed hold of my sleeve and tugged at it. "What team do you play for?"

"The underdogs."

It's funny because I meant it. It went over Bruce's head and he continued to laugh and snort. "You're dressing more like me now."

"I'm dressing the way I want."

"Do you want to be me?"

He always joked about that, ever since we were little and played "army" with pinecone grenades and willow tree whips. He was never serious, but this time, I felt that he sort of was. And I always used to lie and say that I didn't want to when I really did, but this time was different. I thought about it for a few seconds.

"No. I don't."

And it's funny because I meant that too.

"Ya know," he began, "you don't dress like you used to."

"Those clothes don't fit anymore."

Although that was neither a joke nor funny, Bruce started cackling. He leaned back really far in his chair and I couldn't even imagine how he managed to drive from the lake without splattering himself across the road like a Jackson Pollock painting.

The girl in the backseat followed suit and asked if we had any cookies for Santa and I got really annoyed because Bruce went, *"Santa?"* and she leapt into an explanation and it was all too plastic and mindless for me to handle.

"You're such a little liar," he laughed. He then proceeded to wag his finger in my face before I batted it away.

"Get your finger out of my face. I'm driving."

"Bitch, I'll rub my finger all over your clit if I want to."

"Will you knock it off and tell me where this girl's house is?"

"It has brown shutters and a Cadillac in the driveway."

"Thank you. Your detailed directions will lead me straight to her door."

"Calm down. It's on Cottington."

"Cottington?"

"Mhm."

I nodded to let him know that I had heard him. We kept driving past a few houses that looked really expensive. The window shutters were perfectly painted and the garage doors weren't chipped. Every house had backyard gardens and basketball hoops in the driveways.

"She lives in one of these big houses, doesn't she?" I asked, my eyes tracing the picket fences.

Bruce nodded.

"What's she like?" I asked, almost hopeful. "I mean, is she like the others? Or is she, ya know…"

My voice trailed off as the cheerleader emitted a small cry like a distressed kitten. She began hitting her hand on the car window and kicking the back of my seat in a really obnoxious sort of way. I pulled over to the side of the road and she tumbled her way into the grass to vomit.

I gave Bruce a scathing look. "How much did she drink? A tankard?"

"Just leave her here," Bruce told me. "She'll be fine."

"Bruce, don't be stupid."

We sat in silence for a few moments before we heard the gagging cease and the car door open. Suddenly, the scent of spoiled milk wafted throughout the car like fog in summer mornings. The girl was still breathing heavily and slumped across the backseat in such a pathetic sort of way.

I turned off the car. "This is an awful idea."

"What do you mean? It's not like she's going to… to *die*…"

"We can't show up at somebody's house with her being a mess."

"She'll be fine. Come on, I want to go."

"Bruce, it's not all about what you want. I don't think this is a good idea."

"C'mon… it's just one night. I'll look after her and… and you'll have a good time and we'll all have a good time…"

I really should have hit Bruce. I really should have said "no" and turned the car around, but Bruce seemed really set on going to this party. I wasn't a push-over by any means, but Bruce was acting weird because he never begged me to do anything for him that was so ridiculous and he never drove drunk before. He always used to yell at me for driving high. He'd roll his eyes and tell me I was going to be road kill before I hit twenty.

But that night, he was driving around drunk and it was something so out of character that I didn't really know how to handle it. And I *know* that he was an idiot—he always was. I *know* that he was probably the dumbass who you'd expect to drive drunk, and he was dumb as shit, but he c*ared*. That's why he never did it before. He cared a lot about everything because he was the world and he wanted everybody to know it. He cared so much and it was so unlike him to suddenly risk tarnishing his pretty face with a few scars from a smashed windshield.

"Why do you want to go so badly?"

Bruce started fiddling with the radio knob and I thought that, for a moment, I noticed something on his fingers, but he returned his hands to his lap and I told myself that I was just seeing things.

"Because," he began, "I just *do*. It'll be fun. I want to celebrate everything, ya know? I want to celebrate being happy."

My eyes narrowed again and I could have kept asking questions, but I swallowed them all and exhaled in defeat.

"Fine," I said, "but you're taking care of her and you're not going to make an ass out of yourself."

Bruce turned his gaze to the darkness before the car. "Mhm."

"And we're not staying very long because I want to go to sleep. Okay?"

"Yeah, I got it."

"And I'm not going to wait there for an hour while you have shitty, impromptu sex in the pantry like you always manage to do…"

Bruce turned to face me. "Yes, *mom.*"

And the way that he said that pissed me off, it really did. It pissed me off so much because he knew that my Mom was dead and that I always used any excuse to throw up my anger when I heard that fucking *word*. It was so simple, but it rolled off his tongue in such a biting way. "Don't be a little bitch. I'm driving your drunken ass to some party that I don't even want to go to. You shouldn't have brought the cheerleader with you either. I mean, I'm sure she's *great* and all, but she just passed out in your back seat and smells like trash."

His forehead crinkled a bit. Instead of arguing like he always did, he looked stone-cold and ready to keep quiet. With Bruce, that *never* happens, so I took advantage of the moment and unloaded everything that I was frustrated about.

"And you showed up twenty minutes late to pick me up drunk out of your *mind* and you think that it's okay for you to sit there and be just as much of a douche to me as you are to everyone else."

I was disappointed when my last statement was greeted with silence. Bruce continued to stare straight ahead even when I blurted out, "What the hell are you looking at?"

I'm not exactly sure why, but the way he was staring into the darkness was unsettling. I followed his gaze, but I couldn't see anything at all. The heat in the car had begun to escape and we were beginning to see our breath fog up in the air before us like lost ghosts dancing in an empty ballroom.

The cheerleader in the backseat had passed out and Bruce seemed lost somewhere inside his own head. But I wasn't lost. I was still *here*. And I took notice to his eyes. Oh, those *eyes*. They were bloodshot and rounded, entirely still a wax figure's. The blinking streetlamp ahead reflected off his glossy eyes and his cracking lips finally broke open to whisper, "What *is* that?"

I squinted into the darkness in front of the car. I strained my eyes really hard in an attempt to see something beneath that streetlight, but nothing strange was dancing in the darkness or even moving at all.

But something was weird about that darkness. Something wasn't right. Something was off.

The car door opened again, but this time, Bruce stumbled onto the road. I heard the gravel crunch like dead spiders beneath his size 12 shoes.

I was beginning to feel my body temperature drop. My knuckles were probably as white as Bruce's complexion. "What is it?!" I called.

Bruce didn't answer me. He wasn't even looking beneath the flickering street lamp like I had been. Instead, I followed his gaze to a small patch of evergreen trees off the side of the road that were drifting in the fall breeze.

"What are you looking at? Bruce?"

I felt goose bumps crawl down my arms. The radio was coming in and out and Bruce was watching the trees so transfixed that it was all too weird for me.

"Bruce, get back in the car..."

He was backing up slowly, as if somebody were moving around in those trees and he were really afraid. I wanted him to get back inside the car so we could lock the doors and drive away and I'd never have to see what he was looking at.

"BRUCE! GET IN THE CAR!"

He turned. "I just thought I saw... nevermind."

"You thought you saw what?"

He shook his head. "Nothing."

"Is there somebody there? Is there somebody in those trees?"

"No, that's not what I thought I saw. I don't think anything's there..."

And he sat back down in the car and we both sat there for a moment without speaking. Bruce was breathing pretty quickly and I wasn't breathing normally either.

"Chill out. You're being really paranoid for no reason."

He wiped his face on the sleeve of his letterman jacket. "I just thought I saw something, that's all."

"Alright," I whispered. I locked the doors before looking over at Bruce again. His arms were shaking and I suddenly felt really bad for him.

In that very moment, I caught sight of his fingers again and my stomach squirmed because I was right about what I had seen before. His hair was messed up in the front and his face was sweaty and he seemed really off.

"Bruce?" I asked, my voice shaky.

"Yeah?"

I took a deep breath. "Why's there blood beneath your nails?"

Blood. I was so used to seeing it, that I didn't even think that it was real. It was dried and clotted, but I convinced myself that it must've been something else. *It can't be blood,* I told myself. *It just can't be...*

But I knew that it was. And those glossy eyes of his swept over his fingertips and his forehead crinkled again and silence continued to hold us all still like we were in an old photograph. His fingers curled so that I couldn't see the blood anymore and we sat like mannequins or statues in a park.

"What did you... what did you *do*?"

For the first time, I noticed that his jacket had a red stain on the shoulder. He kept staring at me without realizing that I knew it was there. Maybe he didn't know it was there either, but there was something so supernatural holding our gaze onto one another.

"What happened up at the lake, Bruce?"

More ghosts went skyward. I was ready. I was ready to run from the car and never come back. I was ready to cry and disappear forever in the rolling, black hills of the neighborhood. I suddenly wanted my Mom. I wanted to be hugging her goodnight.

It's sad, isn't it? Everyone's mom dies.

Everyone's.

Bruce seemed dirty and grimy all of a sudden and the *only* thing that I wanted to do was clean his fucking nails until they were spotless again, but I knew that doing that wasn't going to make me feel any less dirty.

His lips broke into a faint smile that looked warped. He laughed a little before saying, "You know, you can always trust me..."

I tried to nod, but my neck felt stiff. His smile struck me so off guard that I subconsciously put my hand on the door for security.

He inched forward. "Do you remember how we slept in the same bed during that slumber party and I told you not to tell anybody about it?"

"Bruce…"

He angled his body toward me now. "And do you remember that one time that we threw pebbles at the neighbor's cat until its head was bleeding and left eye didn't open anymore?"

My muscles finally allowed me to nod. Those memories flooded back to me now. Bruce had *insisted* that we sleep in the same bed the night of Michael's party. A few weeks later, we threw all these rocks at Mrs. Herbert's cat until it looked really ruined. That summer was filled with dripping popsicles and ice cream men and following the crowd.

"Bruce," I repeated. "What happened up at the lake?"

"Do you *remember*?"

"Yes…" I stammered. "Yes, I remember."

He leaned back now and my jaw slackened a little bit and my tongue was no longer being pinched between clenched teeth.

"We had so many secrets back then…"

The leather car seat made a really loud cry when he leaned forward, inches from my face. He looked ready to kiss me, but I knew that he wasn't going to do it because things weren't right anymore. Instead, he brought a hand to my face and began running his thumb across my bottom lip.

It just trembled.

"Why are you nervous?" he asked me. "Don't you trust me anymore?"

"Yes…" I mumbled, my voice so weak that I'm not even sure if I said anything at all. "Yes… I trust you."

He pulled his thumb from my lip and shook his head. And that's when he said something that made my bones feel really achy and hollow. That's when he opened his mouth and whispered something so eerie and strange that I just pictured myself running toward the suburban horizon and never finding out the answers.

"I made another secret tonight."

A million thoughts swirled around my head. My breath was all too visible now, blasting from my lips and fading away slowly like fresh, blood droplets in swimming pools.

"What did you do Bruce?"

"I laughed and danced and kissed a girl really long but she doesn't kiss the way you do."

My face crinkled in disgust.

Bruce's laughter carried throughout the car. "I'm just fooling around."

"What *happened*?" I demanded. "Bruce, what the fuck *happened*?"

His laugh faded. "I threw rocks again. I threw a lot of them and broke something that shouldn't have been broken because there was nothing wrong with it at all."

"You broke something? I don't know what you mean…"

Bruce leaned in real close again, his voice a hush. "I threw rocks until it was dead. I threw them just like we used to do back then. And this time, I even understood why I was doing it *less* than I did before."

I opened my mouth to respond, but I couldn't think of anything to say. My jaw hurt really badly and my ears felt really red and sore from the cold that was kissing my skin with too much tongue.

Bruce's cigarette breath made my nostrils flair and he finally said, "But this time, I wasn't throwing rocks at the neighbor's cat."

And silence overtook him and he smiled before opening the door and then slamming it closed. He began strutting down the road with his typical Farrel sway and I just sat in silence with my hands gripping the steering wheel.

When he finally vanished from view, I just cried. I cried because I missed knowing what I wanted and needed. I cried because everybody kept telling me that I was going to make it and shine like Bruce, but I didn't know if I believed them.

They tell me that I'm not going to be sad forever and I cry and whisper, "Do you promise?"

And, in the darkness of that car, I began hitting myself. I left red marks across my face because I just wanted to smack myself until I was clean again. I began digging my fingertips into my neck because I needed to make myself feel better because I *deserved* to be happy.

Lax Hoes, Sports Bros

Dear Lax Hoes and your Sports Bros,

My name is J. Merridew. You may not remember me because this is written under an entirely different name, but I'd just like to let you know that I remember you. In all honesty, I'd never forget you. We all go *way* back. I read your bulletins on Myspace and messaged you on AIM. Chillinpenguin17. That was me. Remember? Anyway, I liked all your pictures and left comments and tried so hard. I was that boy… the one you didn't talk to unless you needed help with math or cramming for an economics test that was so easy to cheat on anyway.

But I guess that's all beside the point now. I don't want to make this any more confusing than it really needs to be. You may be wondering who J. Merridew is because the name probably doesn't ring any bells (we all know that you didn't actually read in high school). Anyway, he's just me, but stronger. He's just me, but less afraid to stand up for what he believes in. He's just a creation to put all of you to shame because finally the loser in high school is cooler than you ever were. You guys never liked me, and I *get it*. I was never into dancing at Homecoming because I felt awkward, and I didn't have girlfriends because I always looked young for my age, and I didn't play football because I didn't feel the need to hit the weight room for hours after class and talk about the Eagles and pussy.

When it all comes down to it, you didn't understand me and I didn't understand you.

And I'm just writing this letter to you to remind you all that you never invited me to your parties. I'd see the pictures and hear the stories, but I never really got an invite. I played on your soccer teams and sat at your lunch tables. I laughed at all your jokes that I didn't find funny. I lied and said that I liked Halo and told you that you looked good in aviators…

It was quite some time ago. I had a bowl cut and you guys didn't have your beer bellies yet. You still had abs and worked out every day after school in the weight room. I was on the honor roll and the only thing you ever rolled was a joint. You hot-boxed in the parking lot and thought that I was a loser and talked shit. It doesn't really matter anymore. I'd just like to let you know that I remember you guys.

So, I want one of you to write back to me. I want *one* of you to explain to me why you never invited me to your parties. That's all that I want to know and I'll shut up and never ask you anything again. I just want to know why you forgot about me because it really sucks, ya know? It sucks to not be invited. And I don't think people get it. Everyone keeps telling me to move on because it's in the past, but that still doesn't make it any better. Moving on won't make me forget about it or make it hurt any less.

Because it hurt. It really did.

And I just don't understand what I was doing wrong.

All of you trophy boys were homecoming kings and I was never in the running. And all of you doll-faced girls were homecoming queens, but I never wanted to dance with you because I was so sick of dancing with girls with small waists and even smaller consciences.

And you never invited me to any of your parties, but it would have been nice to have been invited.

It would have felt nice.

I'd just like to let you know that I dress a bit differently now. I started cutting the sleeves off of those stupid shirts that you guys used to buy. And I started taking pictures of myself lying in confetti and I started throwing up in videos and painting stars on my face and riding around the suburbs on a bike with fake blood all over my nose and writing stories called "Bleach, Blood & Cum" that my mother and grandmother are going to read and shake their heads and say, "What are we going to do with this boy?" And I started becoming this ridiculous, blown-up and extravagant person that seems so sure of everything at the core, but really is just founded off of this never ending desire to prove everybody wrong who never believed in me because so many people don't.

They see a small-town, suburban boy who will never go anywhere. They don't believe in the power of a following. They don't believe that the boy who watched them cry in the rain could make lonely boys and girls like them never cry in the rain again.

If you aren't going to tell your story, I am. People die. Stories don't.

Let's face it. You always thought I'd be the boy who looked like a twelve-year-old and wasn't strong enough to get a crowd cheering on Friday nights. But now... now I'm the boy that you'd die for.

I'm him. I'm just that boy that you'd *die* for.

And if I said that I didn't plan for it to turn out this way, I'd be lying.

And you're all going to think I'm crazy and some of you will hate me for it.

But guess what?

You didn't like me when I was normal anyway, so it's not going to be that big of a loss.

Your glory days ended. You turned in all your cheering and football uniforms and the lights blinked out and now... now it's my turn. Okay? Now it's my turn to be a star because I'm strong too. You talked shit and left me out and bullied me as a kid, and that made me *strong*.

And the moment I start rising, I'm never going to fall because my glory days aren't as temporal as yours were.

I'm not crazy. I just want to be everything. I want to dress vintage frat-boy and bloody *Friday Night Lights,* but not because I want to be like you. I want to be all-American teen spirit and be your wet dream like this underground, suburban sex symbol.

It's because I want to make a joke of it all. I want to make a joke of those glory days because we all know that's all they really were. I'm going to wear old letterman jackets and paint lines beneath my eyes and be this satirical reinvention of you because I just want to make fun of you like you made fun of me.

Because one of these day, I'm going to make it. And when I do, I'm going to have parties with little cocktail wieners that show-up your rockets and we're going to laugh and dance and your invitation is going to get lost in the mail.

I want to be the boy who did it all and said it all and wasn't afraid to dream big because those dream bubbles never pop.

I want to stop feeling so self-destructive.

I want to grow up to be a kid again.

I want to drink up and throw up and stain my white bandana with consumer America.

I want to be your teenage idol.

But I don't want to be perfect and beautiful and infinitely edited with huge arms and six-packs.

I want to just be *wonderful.* I want to stay golden. I want to be brave and unafraid of being myself like so many of the superstars are.

Just let me be your teenage idol. I promise that I'll be the first one that doesn't make you feel... *suicidal.*

Love always and forever,
J. Merridew

PS: I know that you don't deserve this, but I've enclosed something special below. I know what it feels like to miss out on the good parties, so I'm spreading the word. Party on page 92. They're playing the cool-kid music and the punch bowl is ready. I heard Bruce Farrel is going to be there. BYOB. This Friday night is about to get awfully... interesting.

Trophy Boy: Part Three

I hate Bruce Farrel. If I could, I'd kill him and watch him bleed. It'd be so funny to watch him roll around on the floor in his blood and vomit because then I'd feel like I owned him. He'd cry a lot and I'd smile really wide. Everybody thought he bled in gold. The girls thought so. The boys thought so. Everybody thought so.

But I *knew*. I knew that his blood was red like mine. I'd seen him bleed a few times when we were young. He pricked his finger on a nail in the attic and cried. The blood was really dark like roses. He told me to kiss it because his Mom wasn't around and I did. His blood got all over my lips and tasted like pennies. It tasted wonderful.

"It's going to be okay," I whispered. "Everything's going to be okay."

I find myself having dreams of killing Bruce Farrel and watching the blood roll down his high socks. I want his veins to drip red inside his hi-tops and get them really stained and beautiful. I just want to know that he can die. Wouldn't it be amazing? It'd be so stunning to watch blood dribble down his fingertips and neck. When it'd finally crystalize beneath his nails, I'm sure that my lips would have split themselves open in the middle because I'd have been grinning so broadly.

He'd be a bloody mess—like a pig after slaughter. He'd look like I did when I hurt myself and it would be so nice to know that Bruce was just like me when it all came to an end.

I don't want you to think I'm a bad person. I know that pain is awful and blood and guts are bad. I just want to make sure that this world is as fair as they say it is. I want to know that everyone's time here ends in fantasy and my fantasy just happens to be droplets of rubies on Bruce's collar bones.

He'll never know what I did that night. He'll never know that I cried for hours in the front seat of his car. His padding was still somewhere in the trunk and the entire car smelled like stale popcorn at the movies. When my full vision returned, I began wiping blood from my neck because I had hurt myself really badly. Despite spending so much time ripping at my skin, I still managed to straighten-up and clean up like the boys that they advertise in front of the cinema. I pulled my collar up really high because I didn't want anyone to notice the fresh trenches. I laced up my hi-tops and looked perfectly plastic.

As I was fiddling with a lighter, I noticed blood on my fingers. I spat in my hands and rubbed it all around until my fingers were clean. The spit and blood smelled like metal. I wiped it down the side of Bruce's seat before pushing open the door.

Why do I do it? I asked myself, staring into my reflection in the car window.

I don't do it all the time. Please don't think that. Every so often, my stomach gets upset and my face gets really sweaty. When I get that feeling, I need to stop it. I always make sure the nails on my index and middle fingers are clipped in the shape of an upside-down "v" so I can make myself feel better if I ever need to. A lot of people think that it's bad, but I don't think it's that big of a deal. It's just a few scratches. People get scratches all the time.

The plumes of smoke danced in front of me and I tried to grab hold of them because… well, wouldn't that have felt wonderful?

Suck it up, I told myself. *People die and nobody likes the boys who cry.*

I pulled open the door to Bruce's back seat. The cheerleader was still crumpled there like a doll that found its way into a box of doggy toys. "Wake up," I breathed. "Please wake up." I started tapping her cheek with the back of my hand. Her eyes remained closed and her mouth quivered a bit. Some vomit rolled down her chin and into the crevice of her neck.

"Wake up. Please, wake up."

She gargled something in the back of her throat. Her eyelids rolled open to reveal angry eyes concealed with curtains of veins.

"I need you to stay here," I whispered. "Stay here and don't go anywhere."

She didn't give me a nod, only a cloudy gaze. Her tongue slid across the fronts of her teeth, peeling away her dried lips. "Where are you going?"

"I need to find Bruce, okay? You'll be okay."

Before I had finished speaking, her eyes slid closed again and her lips tucked themselves inside her mouth. She made an odd, bubbling sound and then rolled over in her seat and onto the suitcase. "Hurry up."

I slammed the car door behind me. I pulled my bag of purple pills from my pocket and held them up to the moon. I swallowed a few before closing my eyes and taking a few calming breaths. I rubbed the final few tears from my eyes so that these boys wouldn't see me crying. Nobody had to know what I had done in that car. Nobody saw it or heard it. The cheerleader was passed out. Bruce was gone. It was my little secret.

"Pretty, purple pills. All for me."

The cigarette tip was burning lower. The purple pills glided down my throat so smoothly that I could've sworn I was swallowing stars.

"These pills look just like *pearls*," I cried. "Pretty pearls that are going to make me all better."

I was terrified that night, but I was never going to let anybody know it. If anybody were to see me, they would have thought that I was wonderful. They would have swooned and dreamed because my hair looked like I came from Hollywood and my voice was solid again. My neck was red, but I could argue that it came from loving lips instead of a sharpened nail on my pointer finger. People finally thought that I looked like a boy on the television. I looked like a pretty boy, but had the heart of something more and I didn't want people to think that I was as scared as I really was.

After checking my hair in the reflection of Bruce's windows, I blew my nose in some Wendy's napkins from the glove compartment. I headed down the road and through the garden pathways. I knew that Bruce had walked toward the upper development—the one with the larger houses that had backyard swimming pools with spas and pretty lights.

Empty cigarette packets were blowing about the open lawns. There were hamburger wrappers that danced through the hedges like bloody bunny rabbits. I recognized the greasiest ones as the red and white wrappers that the volunteers use at the Coca Cola stand during football games.

The music was faint. I knew that I was approaching the party because there were more cars on the street. A few kids were outside on the porch of one of the houses, smoking bowls beneath cupped hands. Car lights were sending red streaks down the freshly paved streets. There were boys and girls kissing in the back of pickup trucks and laughing inside red solo cups.

The house was beautiful. A large chandelier was hanging overtop the drunken boys who were standing in the open doorway. The golden light bathed them in such a beautiful radiance like false halos over little devils. They gave me a look of amusement as I marched up the driveway, breathing heavily with my head down low. I remember feeling really transparent as I walked toward them. I remember feeling like they could call out my bluff in a matter of moments because my eyes were still wet and my lips were quivering the entire time.

I wanted to kill all of them. Every last one of them. I wished, in that moment, that I had a gun at hand because I would have wedged bullets between all of their gloating eyes. There would have been so much torn skin, but probably no blood at all because dolls can't bleed. Statues and pieces of art just break into smaller pieces of rubble.

As I walked up the steps and into the bright glow of the foyer, I imagined blood-stained walls behind heads that looked like Swiss cheese. I wanted to see porcelain skin shatter and crack like broken china dolls.

A boy can dream, right?

I ran a hand through my hair. When I saw my murky reflection in the birdbath beside the porch stairs, I sighed in relief because I looked so wonderful despite feeling so alone. I always wanted to look perfect, even if I didn't feel so perfect on the inside.

I'm not sure if my eyes were red with tears when I stepped over the threshold and into that party. The girls maneuvered out of my way with wonder in their eyes. The boys gave me incredulous looks that almost came across as worried.

They were worried. I know they were. They were worried because they knew that something was wrong.

"Where's Bruce?" I called down the hall, trying to sound forceful. "Where's Bruce?!"

One of the boys put a hand on my chest to stop me. He retracted it immediately when my gaze met his and my eyes sparked like flint.

"I need to find Bruce," I growled. "I'll leave your stupid party as soon as I find him."

"What's that on your…" he whispered. "What's on your-"

I ignored him. As my eyes swept across the crowd of mannequins in the hallway, I felt my stomach twist and writhe like a sea monster in shallow waters. There was loud music and balloons. The Skye terrier was barking at the foot of the beer pong table in the corner of the living room.

"Where's Bruce?!" I shouted again. "GUYS! Where is Bruce?!"

Somebody in the other room shouted something back at me that I couldn't hear and the awful dubstep from down the hall croaked to silence. The only sound that could be heard was the shuffling of uncomfortable feet on the tile flooring. There was confused chatter from the other room and stifled laughter from drunken girls who were being tickled by boys on regal couches that were being stained with expensive, American puke.

"Where's Bruce?" I repeated. I pushed my way past a boy wearing an awful shirt with clashing tie. "Where is he? Has anybody seen him?"

The longer the silence, the warmer my face became. I felt sweat beneath my eyes and along my hairline. The ends of my lips felt heavy. The more these boys and girls stared at me without speaking, the more anxious I became. I absentmindedly started scratching at my neck, but ripped my hand away because I could feel blood.

It's just a little bit of blood, I told myself. *No big deal.*

But when I brought a hand to my neck again, I started to panic because there was more blood than I had thought and I could feel it pumping from deep gashes that were much deeper than I had imagined. I pulled my hand from my neck and a few people gasped when they saw all the red that I thought had been hidden so carefully.

But it hadn't been. I was bleeding out.

Don't cry, I told myself. *Not here. Don't let them see you hurting.*

"Where is he? I need to know. Where's... where's Bruce?"

And when nobody answered me again, the feeling came back. The girls in the other room continued to giggle while being tickled, and I could've sworn that they were laughing at me. My face got sweatier and more twisted. When I caught my full reflection in the bathroom mirror, I saw the blood-- *all* of the blood. It had soaked through my collar and was running down my neck and polluting the white of my t-shirt like gauze in a dentist's office. I quickly tried to zipper up my jacket to conceal it.

"I need to know guys!" I shouted, embarrassed. "I *need* to!"

"What… what happened to you?"

"Nothing… nothing happened."

I felt a hand on my shoulder now. One of the girls peeled away the collar of my jacket and exposed the broken skin on my neck. They all gasped like they were watching a freak show at the circus.

And I was angry at them for touching me, but even angrier at myself because I had gone too far this time.

"*Let go of me!*" I shouted, pulling my jacket from her hands. When I spun around, I collided with a taller boy and fell to my knees. The fallen beer bled through my jeans and I couldn't help but start to wheeze. "I know we don't get along and you guys don't like me, but this isn't about me. Things… things just aren't funny anymore and I need to know where I can find him-"

Somebody put their hand on my shoulder. I don't know why, but it was too late for any of that. It was too late for apologies and forced comfort.

"DON'T TOUCH ME!" I hollered. "NOBODY TOUCH ME!"

There was more shuffling of imported, European shoes. My skin was tingling because I just wanted to leave this stupid party and never be seen by any of these kids again. They saw my blood, and as badly as I wanted to see theirs, I could never manage to catch them while they were down and they kept seeing me on the floor *over* and *over* again.

"Get him water," one of the girls said. "He needs some water."

"I'm not drunk," I said, wiping tears from my eyes. "I'm fine. I just need to find out where Bruce went because people are looking for him…"

A few boys who were standing in the doorway helped me back to my feet. They brushed off my dirty sleeves. "He left," they told me. "Don't worry about him. He kept saying he needed to go for a walk."

"A walk? Where?"

"He said that he left something back at the stadium."

I was about to force my way past them when one of them stuck out an arm. "You're *hurt*. You're bleeding really badly and you shouldn't go anywhere because you need help."

I tried to wriggle my way though. "Listen, I'm *fine*. Thank you. Enjoy your party."

"Somebody should call an ambulance."

"No, I don't need an ambulance. It's just a little bit of blood…"

The boy didn't lower his arm. He continued to barricade me from the door and I was beginning to feel the monster in my stomach writhing again.

"Let me go… I need to go. Let me fucking go."

"Stop!" one of them shouted, grabbing hold on my other arm and forcing me against the wall. "You're not leaving! You're not okay!"

"Let go of me!" I screamed. "LET GO OF MY ARM!"

My fist collided with the side of a boy's face and the following splash meant that he had fallen into the puddle of beer. My knuckles broke immediately, but my body was numb.

"NONE OF YOU CARED BEFORE! BUT NOW… NOW THAT YOU *SEE* IT, YOU THINK YOU CAN MAKE IT BETTER, BUT YOU CAN'T! YOU JUST *CAN'T!*"

There were screams now and I knew that it was time to leave. Expensive china and family portraits shattered across the floor and the terrier started yelping. My arms were free now. In the panic, more and more kids began filing into the hallway from the surrounding rooms like army ants. I saw their eyes widen and grow when they realized that a boy was lying on the floor with a broken nose, but I was the one bleeding and the scene was just so strange and didn't make any sense at all. A few girls tried to help the boy to his feet, but I wasn't done shouting or throwing things about the hall.

"I WASN'T OKAY LAST YEAR! I WASN'T OKAY HOMECOMING NIGHT… OR… OR *LAST WEEKEND!*"

My eyes were wild. I whipped crystal figurines at the hallway mirror and watched my reflection break into spider eyes across the floor. With all of the chaos whirling around me, I pressed down so hard on my temples until I could breathe right again. The sea monster was biting at the sides of my stomach. It was breathing fire and gnashing its teeth and I didn't know how to stop it.

"I've never been okay," I cried. "Don't you understand? DON'T YOU SEE?! I've always been hurt. I'm hurting every single day, but that never stopped your parties before."

And with that, I slammed the front door behind me and hurried down the stairs. I brought a hand to my hair and began fixing it again while I trudged overtop discarded solo cups and broken cans. I buttoned up my varsity jacket so nobody could see the blood anymore, pulled out a cigarette, and began puffing on that as I walked through open laws again in search for Bruce's parked car.

"BRUCE! BRUCE ARE YOU OUT HERE?!"

I was ashamed of how weak my voice had become. When I had called Bruce's name again, I sounded like an old, wound-up toy at the bottom of a toy chest. I was embarrassed at how I couldn't stop crying and I didn't really know why I couldn't.

After every pathetic shout, the lonely hills gave me no response. The familiar hamburger wrappers continued to dance about the open lawns beside discarded milkshakes from local diners. I heard boys shouting my name from further up the hill. They sounded angry. In a matter of moments, I was pushing my way into Bruce's car.

The voice that sounded from behind was weak. "Did you talk to Bruce?"

I turned. The cheerleader was awake now, her eyes as wide as the crazed terrier back at the house. I twisted the key in the ignition and the engine roared into life. The beats of house music began thundering throughout the car. "No. We're going to find him now."

She sat up. My eyes flashed to the rearview mirror and I could see her gripping the sides of her head. "He came by a few minutes after you'd left."

"He did?"

She nodded. "He took the suitcase. I just want to go home. Take me home."

"I can't."

"You can't?"

"We need to find him…"

"It's on the way, I promise."

A silence hung between us that quickly grew uncomfortable.

"Are you alright? Have you been crying?"

I shook my head. "No, I'm fine. Everything's always fine. I'll drop you off at your house."

Her face didn't slacken, but her lips closed. She shivered a few times. I felt awful watching her shaking in her shirt with vomit frozen down the front. I wanted to give her my jacket, but it was soaked with blood and I didn't want her to see me broken too.

I don't remember the drive to her house. I wish I could. Even now, I'm trying so hard, but all I remember is high beams on stop signs and shitty dance music. The entire ride, I tried to cover my eyes because I could tell she was watching me from the rearview mirror. When she finally rounded the car after I had parked, she knelt down and told me to roll down the window.

"Good luck," she said. "I'm sure he couldn't have gone far."

"Yeah," I breathed. "I'm sure he couldn't have."

The headlights danced across the grass as I began backing out of her driveway. Instead of going inside of her house, the girl waited at the steps of her porch and watched me go. The lights illuminated her vomit-covered shirt and short skirt.

And as I was driving away, she blew me a kiss. I'm not sure why, but I know that her kiss is important to this story in some way. When I figure out why, I'm sure that I'll feel a little bit better.

Suck it up, I told myself, *people change and nobody likes the boys who can't.*

There's nothing like empty suburban roads and lights when you've taken a few pills and your eyes are wet. The lights burst like fireworks overhead and sparkle with such beauty and elegance. Have you ever seen fireworks bursting over suburbia? If you haven't, it's the most beautiful thing in this world because it means that somebody made it.

The parking lot of the stadium was dead. The drinking had ended there long ago. Empty PBR cans were scattered around and the entire thing just looked like a black swamp. The bubblegum pop inside the car whined to silence along with the engine. I pushed my way out of the car before heading up the hill to the stadium.

"Bruce! Bruce where are you?!"

The lights were out. The Coca Cola truck was closed down. There were no starry-eyed mothers with big dreams for their trophy boys. There were no volunteers handing out Twizzlers or overpriced corndogs. A few candy wrappers tumbled across the grass like tumbleweed. I didn't need to hop the fence because the gates were swinging open on their rusted hinges.

"Bruce! Bruce, are you here?!"

The frosted grass of the field crunched beneath my shoes. I came to a halt at the 20-yard-line. The field goal was staring me dead in the face and the scoreboard was dark. I turned left, then right. I walked along the bleachers. I climbed to the top of the stands and surveyed the empty field.

Nothing. Just frozen grass, empty beer cans and a cold wasteland.

It was strange seeing the field so empty. The stands were vacant. There were no cheering high school kids or drunken pre-teens dancing like little goblins. There was just emptiness on that field and it felt like it held so many dreams and memories that I couldn't help but feel oddly insignificant.

"BRUCE!"

My echo bounced off the opposite line of bleachers. I saw dirty confetti and streamers and it made me feel so strange that this little world of ours was ending. I wondered if Bruce knew that his world was ending too. He ran the world now, but were people going to be looking for him after all our graduation hats rained down, or were they going to be moving on? Everybody said he shined and glistened, but why didn't he look that way to me? Why couldn't he be golden for me too? What was wrong with me?

He was nothing that I needed him to be and that's what upset me the most. The night that I needed him more than anything, he was with a girl named Alyssa. He called me a few days later when I wasn't in school to tell me that she had given him head and let him feel her chest for a few minutes after the team won against Palmerton.

"They must love doing it," he told me. "Girls must *love* it. All I have to do is tell her to meet me and she does."

"Meet you?" I asked, hardly listening.

"Yeah, I just told her to meet me beneath the bleachers."

And suddenly, as I stood atop the stands, staring out at the vast emptiness of the football field, I knew where Bruce was hiding.

***

I fantasized about so much blood that night. I had asked to see it running down the stomachs of pretty boys and soaking into the expensive haircuts of skinny girls. I had wanted to see it splattered on walls, between floor tiles and even in the air.

Blood is beautiful. Really, it is. It's so pretty if you can ignore the fact that it comes from inside of you. If you ever have the opportunity, cup some in your hands and slide it all around. It'll harden like wax on your fingertips. It'll get really sticky like glue.

As I was ducking beneath the bleachers, I remember wondering what was waiting for me down there. I had asked to see blood. I wanted to see it everywhere, but as the night had progressed, the only things that I wanted to see were Saturday morning cartoons and sugary milk at the bottom of an empty cereal bowl.

I didn't want blood and guts anymore. I didn't want to see hacked off limbs of prom queens and frat boys. I just wanted to be back at home with my Mom.

"Bruce?" I asked, my voice soft. My warm breath danced before me in that cold air as I sank further into the shadows. My eyes weren't adjusted to the near-complete darkness. All that I could see were small slits of light above me from where the moon was shining through the gaps in the bleachers.

"Bruce… I can hear you. I hear you breathing."

I knew he'd be here. Bruce may have been big. He may have been funny and good at being what everyone wanted, but he was predictable.

"Where are you? This isn't funny. I… I just want to go home."

Silence fell again. I squinted ahead. I held my breath for a few moments in order to better hear where his breathing was coming from. My frown deepened because I realized that I didn't hear his breathing after all.

I heard *crying.* Bruce was crying down there and I hadn't heard him cry since back in grade school.

"Who is that?!" he demanded. "Who's coming?!"

"Bruce… it's me."

"Don't come closer. I'll… I'll fight you!"

"It's Cody!" I shouted. "It's me."

"Cody?"

"Yes, Cody."

When I was close enough, he pulled me into a hug. I needed to grind my teeth together to stop myself from screaming because his hug pulled at the cuts on my neck and they still hadn't scabbed over. The blood was still running down my collar like syrup running down the sides of pancakes.

"It's going to be okay," I whispered, my eyes watering. "Let's go back home. Please, let's just go home…"

I felt him shaking his head.

"Bruce, it's *freezing*. Your hands are so cold. We should go."

Just as I said that, I realized that Bruce wasn't alone. There was a person crouching a few feet away in the shadows. The moment that I noticed, I leapt back like a frightened kitten.

"I didn't know you were with somebody here. I… I thought you were alone!"

Bruce shook his head. The way that he stared back at me made my stomach hurt. His eyes were larger than the moon and they were wet and pink. The pupils were so dilated that blackness had swallowed up so much of the white.

"You didn't have to come," he told me. "You know that, right?"

I nodded. "But I'm your best friend. That's what I'm meant for."

And even as I said it, I wondered why I always told him that I was his best friend, but never told anybody that he was mine.

"What are you doing down here?" I asked. "I swear to God, if you're hooking up with some stupid girl and I spent all night looking for you-"

He didn't answer me. Instead, he turned and started feeling around for something that I couldn't see.

"Bruce!" I stammered. "Tell me what's going on!"

When he straightened up, I saw that he was holding the black suitcase that he had taken from the car. When he opened it, the moonlight reflected off the fronts of a dozen trophies. They were so golden and beautiful. There were plaques and medals. The red and blue ribbons twirled around each other and looked like a Christmas wreath. The gold sparkled and I couldn't stop myself from cupping one of the medals in my hand.

His name was engraved across the back. "BRUCE FARREL." I ran my fingers along the lettering. "Why'd you bring all your trophies out here? Who are you showing them to?"

He didn't answer. Instead, he said, "Help me. Help me with them. Help me put them in his hands and all around him."

"Help you? I don't know what you mean…" My eyes shot over to the black mass along the floor. "Who is that, Bruce? Who's lying over there?"

"I've been here for so long," Bruce whispered. "I've been walking around and putting the trophies all around him because he can't just die here, ya know? At least now, he'll die a boy in gold. You hear me? He'll die a boy in *gold.*"

My stomach began to sink. My eyes flickered over to the black heap again and I was trying so hard to understand what Bruce was saying. I couldn't make out who was crouched in the corner because it was still too dark and Bruce kept handing me trophies.

"Give me that medal," he demanded. "It's the biggest one." He took it from my fingers and replaced it with a smaller one. "Help me," he begged. "Please, help me."

"Listen," I said, my voice rising. "You're not making sense. Help you *what?*"

More tears bubbled up in his eyes. "Put it around his neck."

"Put it around his…?"

I brought a hand to my own neck. It felt tender and broken.

"Don't just stand there!" Bruce shouted. "Help me fix this!"

When I could finally see through the darkness, I saw everything. I saw the blood. I saw the boy on the floor, surrounded with Bruce's old football trophies. It all became so clear to me and I shouted and leapt backward.

"Bruce…. Bruce what did you do?!"

"It's just…" he wheezed. "It's just so hard to breathe when you're made of gold. It's just so hard."

He pulled me into his arms again. My back felt close to breaking and I wanted him to stop. I just wanted everyone to let go of me because I couldn't handle seeing broken superstars and dead boys even when I kept asking for it.

I'm not sure if I imagined it or not, but I could suddenly smell the scent of metal from all the blood. I got sick. It all blasted out of my nose and down my front like that cheerleader in Bruce's car. Suddenly, I wanted her company. I wanted to be with her again because I was younger back then, even if only by a few minutes.

"Bruce..." I cried. "Bruce, what happened?!"

"He was my friend. I don't know what else to do. I just brought all of these trophies and medals here because I don't know how else to make things better-"

"He's... he's dead Bruce. He's fucking *dead*."

"And... and he's just *lying* there now on the ground and nobody else came back for him because nobody cared about him or anything-"

I closed my eyes because I couldn't handle seeing the crumpled boy anymore. The vomit oozed down my front was soaking into the cuts on my neck and burning really badly. I pressed down really hard on my temples with my fingers like I had done back at the party because I felt the monster inside of my stomach beginning to awaken.

"-And I don't remember who started it, but once they started doing it, it just happened because it's so easy to go along. It's just so *easy-*"

"Bruce... he's so bloody and... and..."

"-And he won't wake up and I keep trying and I don't know what to do. I don't know what else to do, so I need you to help me!"

My eyes flickered between Bruce's teary eyes and the boy's broken ones.

"HELP ME!" Bruce shouted. "DON'T JUST STAND THERE, HELP ME!"

"I don't know how to *help*," I cried, my tears matching his. "You can't fix this. This isn't something where you just smile and pretend that nothing happened!"

"I'm not pretending that nothing happened! I can't do that…"

"This is something *bad*. It's something so bad and you can't change it!"

"Then how do I make myself better?!"

"You do what I do! You take pills! You don't do *this!*"

I gestured to the boy who was curled up in the shadows. But when I saw the blood on the ground, and raised a hand to the blood on my neck, I wondered if there was even a difference. I dug a hand in my pocket to see if I still had the baggie of manufactured warmth. When I felt moist, empty plastic, I realized I only had a handful of pills left inside.

Pretty, purple pills. So pretty and beautiful. They shine just like *pearls*. Pretty, purple pearls that are all for me.

Bruce's voice had fallen now, no longer a shout and more of a plea. "Please help me. I can't let him die down here surrounded with flies and… and broken *dolls*. I just can't."

I swallowed a few. They fought their way down my scratchy, dry throat.

"CODY, TELL ME WHAT TO DO! HELP ME!"

"I CAN'T BRUCE! I JUST CAN'T!"

"WHY NOT?!"

"BECAUSE!" I shouted back. I stopped to take a deep breath. "Because I don't *want* to."

He just stared at me. He wasn't expecting me to say that. He was expecting me to cry for him and hug him, but I wasn't going to do that anymore.

"You don't want to?"

I saw his warm breath vanish into the air along with the "want to." As it slipped from his lips, I couldn't stop myself from clenching my fists and grinding my teeth together. It numbed my stomach and boiled my blood. He wanted *my* help— help from the boy who was always fighting so hard to be perfect and beautiful, but never could shine because no light ever makes it into the shadows. He wanted help from the boy that he gave nothing to.

"Help me…" he repeated. "Help me, Cody. I have to make it better…"

And I wanted to bust his head open. Just like back at the party, I pictured screaming and bloody mouths. I wanted to break his face because it wasn't fair. I wanted to rip him apart like an animal and pull out his baby blue eyes like oysters from a shell. I hated him so much in that moment because I was bloody and covered in vomit with a broken hand and he wanted *my* help. A single tear trickled down my cheek, but this time, it wasn't from sadness. I was no longer sad in that moment because I couldn't pity him. More furious tears fell down my face because Bruce never stopped to try to fix things with me because I wasn't his mess to fix.

"I want to show you something."

And with that, I removed my letterman jacket. It crumpled to the cold macadam like a fallen parachute. The cold air licked at my cuts and made them feel really numb. I wanted him to see it. I wanted him to see all the red because Bruce never realized that people actually bleed. He never noticed anything and that's why I hated him so much.

His eyes traveled down my neck. I saw them trace the deepest cuts on the side and below the chin. As we stood there that night, shivering beneath the bleachers, he saw everything that I tried so hard to hide.

"What happened to you?"

"Do you see them?" I asked, twisting my neck. I brought a finger to the longest one that reached down my chest. "This one's my favorite."

"What happened to you?" he repeated. "That's not funny. What happened?!"

I let out a laugh that quickly melted into more tears. "Where were you, Bruce?"

More of his breath twirled toward the sky, but no sound escaped his lips. He didn't know what I meant, and it didn't surprise me because he didn't even understand how to put two and two together on math quizzes freshman year, so how would he know how to do it now?

"Where were you, Bruce?"

"When?"

"When my mother died? Where were you when I called you that night? How about when I wasn't in class all week and had to quit playing football because I needed to spend time with my dad?"

Silence.

"Where were you?"

"I don't know," he whispered. "I… I don't know where I was…"

"OF COURSE YOU DON'T!" I bellowed. "OF COURSE YOU DON'T REMEMBER BECAUSE YOU WEREN'T WHERE YOU WERE SUPPOSED TO BE!"

His face fell. He still had those *stupid* trophies in his hands that he thought he could use to make things better. He had this hurt look across his face, like a little boy who didn't understand and I couldn't stand to look at him anymore.

"AND I NEEDED YOU SO MUCH BECAUSE I WASN'T READY FOR IT AND YOU WEREN'T THERE! YOU WERE MY BEST FRIEND AND YOU WERE GONE AND NOW YOU WANT MY HELP AND IT'S NOT FAIR! IT'S JUST NOT FAIR!"

When I gave him time to respond, he said nothing and just stared at me with that dumbass expression he pulled off so well.

"SAY SOMETHING!" I hollered. "SAY SOMETHING BECAUSE I'M SO SICK OF NOBODY KNOWING ANY ANSWERS! I'M SO SICK OF SEEING PEOPLE DIE BEFORE THEY'RE MEANT TO AND I'M SO SICK OF NOTHING BAD EVER HAPPENING TO THE PRETTY BOYS! IT'S NOT FAIR, IT'S JUST NOT FAIR!"

He started fumbling for words. "I... I don't know what to say…"

A fresh batch of tears glided down my face. "You *had* to have known. She came to every one of our games, Bruce, *every* one until she couldn't anymore. After every game, she'd hug me and tell me that I was going to be a *star*."

Bruce nodded before looking down. "I... I think I remember."

I rubbed my eyes. "But look at me now. She'd be real proud, wouldn't she? Wouldn't she Bruce?"

And when he looked up, he didn't answer because there was nothing for him to say.

"Look at me now," I sobbed, running a hand down my scarred neck. "Some star I turned out to be, huh?"

As I released my final sigh, I felt the monster in my stomach calm. It curled up somewhere and went to sleep because I wasn't mad anymore. I was just disappointed in Bruce because he was nothing when I needed him to be everything.

When I looked back at him, I didn't imagine bullet holes anymore. He had a really worked-up expression on his face, almost like he was holding his breath for too long. He was staring down at the ground the way he used to stare down at Algebra tests. His big fingers were shaking around the trophy he was holding and he kept spinning the medal around in his fingers. Instead of wishing for blood, I just wished that he'd sparkle like the trophy boy he was meant to be.

"I'm sorry, Bruce. I can't help you anymore. I can't be a part of this. This is… this is just too much."

And when I shook my head in further disappointment and began to walk back the way I'd come, he lifted his head up and said something that I'd never forget.

"You're a star to me."

I stopped. I was so surprised that I didn't breathe for a moment or two.

"What did you say?" I asked, turning.

"I said that I think you're a star," he whispered, his forehead crinkling. "And I know that I'm not always the nicest guy to be around, and I'm not smart and I don't know how to make people feel better, but I… I…"

He ran his fingers through his hair in frustration, almost like a toddler who was trying so hard to speak, but couldn't find the right words.

"Listen, I know that things change, but not everything changes. I know you're hurting and I don't know what to do to make it stop, but I think I can make it a little bit better if you'd just let me try. I can fix things. I can fix everything that I've screwed up."

"Fix things?" I said with a laugh. "You think you can fix things?"

"I'm not as *dumb* as everybody thinks, okay? I know what everyone says about me, but I'm not always like that."

"Alright," I nodded. "Alright, Bruce. Fix things."

He let the trophies fall from his hands. "I just have an idea about what to do because it's the first thing that I thought of. It's probably stupid and you're just going to laugh, but I think it can help because it always worked before for me."

"What's the idea?"

He took a few steps toward me. His teeth were chattering because it was so cold and his hands were shaking too.

"Close your eyes and think about when we were little."

"Bruce," I laughed, "I'm not going to *close* my eyes…"

"Cody, just *try it*. Okay? Don't laugh and just try it because it could work if you'd just *try*."

I sighed and squeezed my eyes shut.

And I just stood there for a few moments in the freezing cold with a blank mind. After a bit of thinking, I began imagining myself running through open lawns and jumping on beds during slumber parties. And when I was just about to open my eyes because I felt so stupid, I felt something on my neck that I wasn't expecting.

I wasn't expecting it at all. I was expecting to feel the constant stinging of cold air inside my warm wounds, but I felt something much different.

I felt kissing.

Bruce was kissing every last one of those cuts with his trembling lips. He kissed all the open ones on my neck just like I had done for him back when we were young and playing in the attic.

"It's going to be okay," he whispered. "Everything's going to be okay."

He kept kissing and kissing and when he was done, he looked at me and said, "You see? Not everything changes." And then he pulled me into a hug and said, "I'm glad that I have a best friend like you."

And I didn't need to say anything because we both knew.

I will never forget that night. I will never forget Bruce Farrel. I'll never forget our hometown hero because I met him that night for the first time and it was wonderful. He became the trophy boy that I always needed him to be, and he didn't even need a football or solo cup to do it.

Made in the USA
Lexington, KY
27 January 2016